Deep

Dark

By Brian Bargmann

Paperback: First Edition
ISBN-10: 1940752000
ISBN-13: 978-1-940752-00-6

E-book Edition
ISBN-10: 1940752019
ISBN-13: 978-1-940752-01-3

Published by Creative Machinations
Cover Art by David Hickerson
Cover Design by Brian Bargmann

Prologue

Humanity's first endeavor into space began with the launching of Sputnik One in 1957. That event marked the beginning of the Space Age. It was also the opening gambit of the Soviet Union's space race with the United States, which would finally prove which nation was superior. However, a century later, the space community in the twenty-first century identified the 1960s as the dawning of the first space era. It began with humanity's first voyage in a manned spacecraft into space. Later, humanity journeyed to the earth's moon and explored its surface. Now, the biggest debate is when the first space era ended and when the second era began. The most popular view of the first era ending, is with the abandonment of the International Space Station in the early twenty-first century. The second era began with the completion of the first industrial complex in space. This sparked the beginning of the commercial space race. Everyone agrees that an era definitely ended in the 2070s. The lack of resources and new technologies led to a stagnant period in space endeavors. Despite the breakthrough and the development of the antimatter reactor in 2083, a new space era did not begin until the beginning of the twenty-second century. In 2104, the first light-speed engine was developed and prompted a new race. In 2115, a new platform was developed called a star catapult. It allowed ships equipped with debris screens to be launched at light-speed instantly and safely. Within the next five years, three corporate-sponsored exhibitions were assembled and launched, using the new star catapult, to three different systems. Even at light-speed, it still took them years to reach their destination. Their main goal was to establish a human presence in their corresponding target systems. They hoped was to discover a planet that was suitable for human colonization. However, they had designed their fleet of ships to connect and form into a space station. The space station would then form as their base of operations while they surveyed, explored, and experimented. The news of the exhibitions created new excitement over the prospect of discovering new worlds to be colonized. This marked the beginning of the new era: the Third Space Era.

Chapter 1

Inside Asteroid Tangent, Home of Tony
Black

Ethan Burnet looked up as he heard his roommate, Tony Black, stumble and stagger out of his bedroom and slowly move toward the bathroom. Ethan shook his head, laughed, and said, "Good morning, boss." Tony ignored him and closed the hatch to the bathroom. A little while later, Tony exited and headed to the dining room, where Ethan was still sitting and watching the morning news on the holovision in the center of the table in the dining room.

Without taking his attention away from the news, Ethan started talking. "Do you realize that if you could function properly after waking up from sleep you would probably be an officer by now-maybe even a general."

Tony sighed and said, "That is very unlikely. Besides, I do not want to be an officer." This got Ethan's attention.

He looked up and asked, "Why do you not want to be an officer?" Tony grabbed some food and sat down.

"It is simple. Officers have a lot of responsibilities and those responsibilities are very time-consuming. Plus, the way the current military structure is configured for the marines, commissioned officers are stationed only on the bases or the outposts. Noncommissioned marine officers are the only ones who have duties on marine spacecraft. I love piloting assault crafts. It can be very exciting when we have to board another ship. Normally, though, as soon as I get the assault craft away from the areas of heavy traffic, I am free to engage the autopilot and do whatever I want, as long as it is within reason."

Ethan smirked at this last comment and replied, "I wondered how you were able to be a marine and still manage the affairs of your billion-credit company." Tony shrugged, got up out of his seat, and took his dishes to the dishwasher.

After he was finished, he returned to his seat and replied, "Actually, I do not really run the company anymore. I hired other people to take care of the corporate management functions. I have been doing this ever since I started selling items with integrated gravity tech on the open market. I had a feeling the company would need to expand quickly, so I planned ahead of time. I am still focused on incorporating the gravity tech into new products but I am also developing other technologies." Tony saw from Ethan's facial expression and posture that he felt dejected. Tony chuckled. Ethan scowled and was about to snap at him.

Tony said, "Relax. I have not forgotten about our plans to restart the galaxy exploration program. In fact, I've been discussing it with Brigadier General Thomas, Rear Admiral Shelton, and Vice Admiral Colder. They seem interested in my ideas, but they are not yet ready to promise anything in the way of help at the moment. Well, Brigadier General Thomas is willing to still help with the company and to aid us in extracting refugees from the corporate systems. As far as the exploration project goes, the main problem right now is transportation."

Ethan interrupted him by asking, "How is transportation the main problem?" Tony glanced at Ethan, disappointed and exasperated with him for not considering what their current issues with space exploration entailed.

Finally, he replied, "I know you have only been back in human space for a year now. However, despite returning through the wormhole and being dumped out forty years later than you expected, I thought you would have given this matter more thought. Despite meeting the Nubians, we are still limited to light-speed drives for exploration. As you well know, the closest unexplored systems that we know about are over a decade away. Naturally, no one really wants to endure that long of a trip, especially since the outcome is so uncertain and we have not yet discovered any habitable planets." Tony waved toward the holovision, where the host of a news show and two guests were discussing the riots and protests that were currently occurring in several nations. "Unfortunately, Tony continued, "people are unhappy that we were not able to find any habitable planets, and so far the terraforming of Mars has failed three times. However, you have already heard my rants about the terraforming of Mars." Ethan smiled sadly and nodded. Tony continued, "Well, our first major hurdle for space exploration is finding a method for moving instantaneously or faster than the speed of light. I think the answer lies with technology that is similar to what the Nubians use. I have not been able to discover whether their ships use the same technology as the gateways, but I hope to find out soon. I am planning to figure out the scientific principles that they use. Hopefully, I will be able to devise a method for making it work with our current knowledge and technology. I think that once it becomes less time-consuming to travel to new star systems, I will have an easier time convincing the military and/or the United Earth Federation to restart our efforts to explore outer space." They remained quiet as they watched the holovision and thought about future space exploration.

Finally, Ethan asked, "Why do you want to involve the military or any government? You might feel a sense obligation to the UEF Marines because you are one of them, but I do not see the need to involve them. I am guessing you are wealthy enough to mount your own expeditions."

Tony nodded, saying, "Yes. I thought about retiring early, but then I started to think about my future plans. I decided to try a different approach. What if one of the expeditions found a habitable planet in a distant system? What if they found another alien species either on a planet or while in transit? Who will deal with new alien contacts? We got lucky with the Nubians. From what we can determine, they are a peaceful species that primarily trades. We are lucky that they surprised us and were able to talk to us soon after they arrived in the earth's orbit. The fear of the unknown has a way of causing us to react rashly by shooting first and asking questions later. Anyway, I came to the conclusion that UEF would have to be involved in some way. Their level of involvement is open to debate. It is not really something that I am worried about right now. Since it is in your area of expertise, maybe you should look into that. There will have to be procedures, rules, and guidelines concerning the exploration of foreign systems, making contact with alien species, and the methods of gathering information. Just follow my method by thinking up every possible scenario that is plausible. You can worry about implausible ones later."

Ethan grunted and replied, "Implausible? Do you mean, like a worm hole popping open right in front of your ship and swallowing you into a nightmare?" Tony winced and nodded somberly.

"Yes, like that. However, I guess it will be good to improvise. I doubt you will want to cover every different aspect and factor involving that event." Tony looked down at the clock that was displayed on the tabletop. It was time to get a move on, so he stood up and headed to his room to finish packing for his trip back to work.

Chapter 2

In the Vicinity of the Sol-Tuscarora Gateway
in the Sol System

Diane cleared her throat and activated her camera in preparation for her first recording on this specific assignment. "Welcome. I am Diane Hope, host of *Galactic Weekly* on the Galactic News Network. On this week's show we are embarking on a journey through the human occupied systems onboard the ship, *Proud Pegasus*. This year celebrates the twenty-fifth anniversary of the establishment of the trade agreement with the Nubian race. I will be interviewing various guests concerning matters related to that momentous event and the current state of affairs." Diane paused for a moment while the camera zoomed out to include the ship's captain and a wall display that showed a visual representation of the traffic in the Sol System. "Currently, we are about to enter the gateway to the Tuscarora System. We will be traveling nine light years in a matter of seconds." The spokeswoman turned to the captain and asked, "Captain Michaels, what is the procedure for entering a gateway?" The captain checked the various screens in front of her and then released her seat so that she could swivel around to face the show's host.

"Well, Mrs. Hope," she said.

Hope interrupted her by smiling tightly and saying, "Please, just call me Diane." Anything that reminded Diane of her marriage, always made her cranky. However, since most of the universe did not know this, they did not know they should avoid any reference to it. So as a result, the captain gave her a frosty smile in return for the interruption.

The captain then resumed her explanation. "Each gateway has a Nubian A.I. attendant that acts as a traffic controller for ships that want to pass through the gateway. To gain passage through a gateway, you need an authorized gateway pass and enough credits to pay the fee."

Diane asked, "What is the pass and who can get one? How does one obtain a pass?"

The captain nodded and replied, "First, anyone can technically apply for a pass but the Nubians must approve your application. Normally, you will have no problems with receiving one if you are a ship captain and you command a ship that is capable of going to the speed of light. The pass basically allows the holder to gain entry into a selected gateway queue after he or she has paid the necessary fee."

Diane asked, "On average, how much is the fee?"

"Currently, the fee for a vessel this size is 2500 credits for gateways in human space and I have heard the gateways to Nubian systems are double that. However, the fee varies depending on the size of the ship. Small vessels pay 250 credits. Medium vessels pay one thousand credits. Large vessels pay 1800. On a side note, the Nubians strictly forbid vessels with weaponry other than short-range weapons. Therefore, most military ships are forbidden from using the gateways."

Diane raised her thin eyebrows and said, "Yes, that has been a major point of contention within the UEF Navy lately. Do you know why the UEF agreed to that arrangement? Do you know if they even planned to have a military at that time?"

The captain rubbed her right temple for a moment and then answered, "Well, to begin with, the UEF and the space navy did not even exist back then. In fact, the Nubians insisted on creating a unified governmental body for the planet before they would even deal with us. A year after the UEF was founded along with its navy and marine contingent, the Nubians returned and opened trade negotiations with the UEF. The short version of that outcome was open trade with the Nubians, within our own borders, in exchange for the Nubians gateways. Which allowed instantaneous travel between star systems. This enabled us to connect to the three other star systems that humans had sent expeditions to earlier. After that, we started to scout out the nearby systems so that the Nubians connect them with gateways. The rest is history, as they say." Diane nodded. Appearing to think of something in particular, she leaned forward with an eager expression that the captain did not like.

Diane answered her fears by asking, "Currently, the corporate systems are discontent and angry about the lack of support from the government, the police, and the military when they are paying taxes to support them. Now, we are headed to your company, Tangiers Limited, which is in the Caledonia System. Does your company feel the same way? Do you think that the corporate systems, including Caledonia, will demand independence from earth or insist on support from earth?" Diane continued to lean forward with eager anticipation. The captain just clenched her jaw. Thankfully, there was a timely interruption from the navigator, who announced that the A.I. attendant was scanning them. The captain took the opportunity to change the subject.

"The A.I. attendant just scanned us to determine our size and weapon load. I have heard that they can scan deeper to determine the number of crew members, passengers, and the type of cargo being transported. However, there are no restrictions on those things, so the attendant scans the outer hull." The communications officer reported on a successive scan. The officer confirmed clearance to transmit the fee and pass data. The captain confirmed the report and entered her pass into a slot on the console in front of her. She then went about transmitting the data and the funds. Thirty minutes later, the *Proud Pegasus* entered the gateway. The ship eased to a stop inside the gateway and the captain announced she was activating the debris screen. The communication officer announced a fifteen-second warning to the bridge crew and then announced a ten-second warning to the ship's entire crew. Out of curiosity and anticipation, Diane fidgeted in her seat. Finally, there was a bright flash and a quick view of a bluish wave of energy crashing toward the ship. Everyone experienced a strange gut-wrenching feeling, and then everything was quiet again. The communications officer announced first to the bridge and then to the entire crew that they were now in the Tuscarora System, and the navigator confirmed the report. Diane took several minutes to recover from the new experience. She was watching the external visuals on the screens when she noticed something odd.

She asked, "Captain, why does this gateway look different?" The captain glanced at one of screens and nodded.

"Ah, yes. I forgot to explain that there are actually two different types of gateways. One is an entrance gateway and one is an exit gateway. I have heard that there are gateways that can serve both purposes, but they are only good in systems with a low amount of traffic." Diane thought about this for several minutes.

"Hmm, then why are the entrances and exit not near one another then and I have noticed the gateway placement in the Sol system is strange for some the gateways. Why is that?"

The captain said, "A lot of science is involved in placing gateways. Simply explained, streams of dark matter connect the various nearby systems. The gateways create artificial wormholes that use dark energy to propel the contents of the gateway through the dark matter stream to a nearby system. Essentially, it is a shortcut that avoids travelling through the space between star systems. From what I understand, it is far too dangerous to have ships passing one another inside the matter stream. So each gateway uses an individual matter stream that is separate from any others."

Diane replied, "Thank you, captain. That was a simple explanation of something that I am sure is very complicated." The navigator reported that they were clear to travel to Tuscarora One, the first and still the primary space station in the Tuscarora System. It was about two days away. The captain confirmed the report and then allowed the communications officer to give the all-clear announcement to the rest of the crew so that they could get back to work around the ship.

Diane excused herself and headed back to her cabin for some sleep. She needed to be well rested to endure the unknown surprises that her auntie, the admiral, had in store for her in Tuscarora.

Chapter 3

Emperor Terminal, Earth, Sol System

A work crew of fifteen men were seated in one of the compartments of the gigantic orbital elevator that overlooked Hong Kong and stretched up to the edge of the earth's atmosphere. After ascending for about two hours, the elevator compartment came to a stop and a recorded message started its presentation in the preselected language of Arabic. One of the bigger men stood and eyed the rest of them. He said, "Remember the instructions I gave you and we will not be noticed by security while we are in the terminal. We only need to reach a private berth on the opposite side of the terminal. There is only one security checkpoint that we will have to pass through, and I was assured that we will not have any problems if we just follow the instructions." The group then made their way down the many corridors to the main annex. The annex was the core of the terminal. It housed the commercial part of the terminal, which included retail stores, restaurants, and public services. Naturally, this was the busiest part of the terminal. It had the biggest crowds. However, just before the group reached the annex, they had to walk through a checkpoint to reach the main corridor. The group got in line for the checkpoint and followed all of the directions to proceed through security. Ten minutes later, the group had made it through the checkpoint with no apparent problems. However, the security system had noted some minor anomalies among many of the fifteen men. The system automatically increased its surveillance on these individuals as they entered the annex. The group had been instructed not to stop in the annex because of the heightened security in that area. The group was three-quarters of the way across the annex when two pairs of lovely long legs got the attention of the youngest member of the group. He reflexively looked up to admire the rest of the two young women. Then he remembered the warning. By then, it was too late. A security camera had seen his face. More notably, it had seen the tattoo near his left eye. A facial recognition program found a match within nine-tenths of a second. The security system noted that this individual was suspected of being a convicted felon and thus should probably not be allowed inside the terminal. Human security personnel were immediately alerted. A minute later, a group of six United Earth Police personnel approached their target head-on. Another group of six police officers approached them from behind. However, the second group was having trouble navigating the sea of people wandering through the annex. They were still twenty-five meters away when the front team confronted the young man. However, the police had miscalculated. They had assumed that the young man was the only threat, even though he was obviously with a group of work men. In a loud and commanding voice, the policewoman in the lead told the young man to stop. Just then, two the bigger workmen sprang into action, charging and tackling the group of police. Four more of the workmen joined in, prying weapons loose from the struggling police while they were occupied with the two giant workmen holding them down. The leader of the workmen barked some orders, and eight of the men grabbed some nearby pedestrians who had stopped to gawk at the disturbance. The loud yelling that was coming from behind them alerted them that a second group of police officers was now nearly on top of them. The four people who had gone for the weapons quickly spread the extra weapons among their nearby comrades. Then they stood near the hostages and started to use the laser pistols that they had stolen from the police officers. Three of the 6 police officers went down immediately under the barrage of laser fire crackling through the air. The other three dove to the ground and returned fire. The entire annex was now quiet and still, except for the charging whine of the weapons. The silence was abruptly ended with the bone-chilling scream of one of female hostages. A bolt of laser fire grazed the side of her head, reducing the man who had been holding her to a headless body with a stub of frying meat. The sight and the sound of the woman screaming and rolling on the ground in agony distracted the spectators from their fascination with the horror. Chaos ensued as stampedes of people erupted in every direction. Meanwhile, the two armed groups continued to exchange laser fire. They were both caught out in the dining area of the food court. The tables and the chairs were the only things to take cover behind, and they were fairly useless against lasers. However, soon enough all of the armed workmen had been eliminated. The six men who held the hostages and the leader were the only ones who remained alive and intact. The leader saw that there were more police officers heading their way. He ordered his men to toss their hostages toward the three police officers who were lying prone on the ground and yelling at them to surrender. After that, they would make a break for one of the main corridors. The main corridors were all currently packed with people who were trying to escape the annex. The six thugs did what they were instructed to do. One of police officers flinched from the sudden attack, and he shot one of the hostages who had been thrown her way. However, when the hostage dropped dead to the ground, one of the other police officers took advantage of the clear line of sight. Three people were running away. With beanbag rounds from his riot gun, he shot them each in the middle of the back. The remaining four gunmen ran toward them. The remaining group of people who were crowded just inside of one of the main corridors panicked and scrabbled to get away from the madmen. The last person made it twenty meters into the corridor when the four men, including the leader, reached the corridor. However, the terminal's security personnel closed and sealed the bulkhead doors at the twenty meter mark as soon as it was clear. The four men had been charging quickly into the corridor, and they had trouble stopping. By the time they realized the danger that they were in, it was too late. Another bulkhead door closed at the end the corridor, trapping them inside. Instead of simply incapacitating the four fugitives, an overly eager security officer had engaged a lethal response. Two laser turrets dropped from the ceiling and fired upon the defenseless men.

Chapter 4

Susquehanna Station One, Susquehanna

Tony Black brought his ship, the *Coldstream*, within range of the docking port, and he signaled to station traffic control that the ship was in position. It was waiting for the mooring grapples to be securely fastened to the hull so that the ship could be reeled into the docking collar. Tony did not waste any time watching the progress of the docking procedures. Instead, he headed back to the docking bay on his ship and prepared his cargo to be unloaded. He periodically checked the progress of the docking through his heads-up display on the inside of the faceplate in his helmet. He also checked the progress by listening to the traffic controllers over the communication channel, which was also audible in his helmet. Tony finished preparing the cargo crates for unloading. The cargo had picked up earlier that day from his company's station, which was also located in the Susquehanna Star System. The crates contained new drones that he was hoping to be able to test soon. He was sick and tired of having to sweet-talk the marine generals into allowing him to use and test the new drones. It was especially troublesome because he was trying to conceal his identity as the owner of the company, Infinite Machinations. The corporations that were not in the Sol System had been on the receiving end of recent hostilities from earth. Naturally, some companies probably deserved it but not all. The United Earth Federation was also displeased with the inhabitants of the Lafayette and Huntington star systems. All of the companies had banded together to create megacorporations in each of these systems. The leaders of the two megacorporations were both threatening to secede from the federation if the UEF did not lower tariffs on goods passing to and from the Sol System. The UEF had been debating these topics for the past couple of years. Meanwhile, the tensions had been escalating the entire time. More citizens of earth were adopting different degrees of isolationism. Some felt that the UEF should only be concerned with the Sol System, while most citizens were only concerned with earth. They felt that the UEF should only focus on their home planet. Regardless, Tony wanted to keep his public and private lives separate as much as possible.

Tony saw that the docking procedure was complete, but he checked with traffic control and got a confirmation before opening the inner hatch in the cargo bay of the *Coldstream*. Tony walked into the ship's entryway, checked the status of the conditions outside, and then opened the outer hatch. A marine private was standing there and waiting for him. Tony was wearing his armored marine space suit. His rank insignia was visible over the right side of his upper chest. The private was surprised to see the marine onboard the civilian ship, but he came to attention after seeing the insignia.

"Welcome to Susquehanna One, master sergeant. I am Private Rollins and I am here to check your manifest and cargo." Black nodded, pulled an electronic pad off of the wall next to the hatch, and handed it to the private for him to examine. He checked it over and then asked if he could examine the cargo. The master sergeant turned, walked back to the cargo bay, and stopped next to the first row of crates. He turned around and watched the private go along the row of crates, scanning the crates and checking the data. Satisfied with the first row of crates, the private made a call over his communication set. A minute later, another private came in with a cargo lifter and started to remove the crates two at a time. One hour later, all of the crates were unloaded. Tony undocked and then docked again at a location where ships were berthed for long-term docking. Tony spent another hour going through the shutdown procedures. Just before disembarking into the station, he activated the onboard defenses for the ship.

The next morning, Master Sergeant Black reported back to duty at a scheduled briefing meeting in the office of Lieutenant Colonel Samantha Howe, who was the commanding officer of the UEF Marine's 23rd Battalion. She was also the overall marine commander of the Susquehanna System. Personally, the master sergeant was feeling a bit apprehensive about the meeting. It was with the highest-ranking marine officer in the system, which was unusual. On the other hand, this was not the first time Black had met with the lieutenant colonel. In the past, he often did this to get a special assignment. Black was a floater in the command structure of the UEF Marines. He was often a technical instructor for the enlisted personnel. Sometimes he was an instructor in tactics. He was sometimes employed as a specialized engineer or advisor, and he was still involved with several long-term projects. As result, Black had been assigned to every platoon in the battalion at least once. However, he was normally just issued new orders with a transfer. He was rarely summoned for a meeting. Upon entering the office and coming to attention just inside the door, the master sergeant was surprised to see the lieutenant colonel. He was also surprised to see Captain Will Moore, who was the leader of E Company, and Lieutenant Cheung, who was the leader of First Platoon, E Company. In a rare display of respect for a noncommissioned officer, all 3 of them stood up and at attention. This caused more discomfort for the master sergeant, but it also increased his curiosity about this meeting. Lieutenant Colonel Howe sat down and waved the other three to the seats in front of her desk. Black was still not sure if he should be appalled or amused by the military discipline and customs of the UEF Marines compared to that of the US Marines. Black had served as a marine for the United States for 10 years before joining UEF Marines, where he now had been serving for almost 22 years. For a comparison, the US Marines is a 100 percent military organization, despite the occasional reforms that resulted from social, political, and religious influences. In contrast, the UEF Marines was a unique amalgamation of government, military, and corporate components. It took some time for people to adjust to this new military organization, and after 28 years the UEF Marines is still functioning.

Lieutenant Colonel Howe started the meeting off by reintroducing everyone and explaining the purpose of the meeting. "I requested this meeting so that we would all be on the same page regarding several matters that have involved or will primarily involve Master Sergeant Black and a certain special squad." Howe paused for a moment, eyeing each of them before continuing and focusing her attention on Black. "First, I would like to update the master sergeant on current events, since he has been on leave for the past month. There were six accidents involving marine spacecraft over the past month, and now we are currently down to just one operational assault craft. A week ago, I received orders to prepare the members of the neural combat interface project for a joint operation with their navy counterparts." Howe paused when she saw the master sergeant shifting in his seat. "Do you have a question, master sergeant?" Black hesitated for a moment.

He then replied, "No. It is just that I was unaware that the navy had a similar program. Now that I know, I cannot help but be concerned about the security of their program, since the security of our own program was seriously breached." Black glanced at the two other officers. Then he looked back at the lieutenant colonel, silently questioning the current state of security. He was not sure whether or not Captain Moore and Lieutenant Chueng had the security clearance to have received a briefing on the program in question. It would have made sense for them to be cleared, but he was unwilling to let something slip before knowing about their security status.

In response to the unasked question, Howe nodded and replied, "Yes. I just got done briefing the two of them on the basics of the program. Yes, the navy has a similar project, but I am unaware of its details. I had to read between the lines of the message, but I think the project encompasses the entire crew of the destroyer *Ravager*, which could include anywhere from seventy-five to one hundred and fifty crew members. Anyway, Vice Admiral Rayner had sent orders for a platoon of marines from Susquehanna. This would probably include all of the participants of the NCI project. Each of the four squads was to be sent in an assault shuttle. As I explained earlier, we currently only have one assault shuttle that is operational. That is our first major problem. Next, the orders explain that the platoon is to partake in a training exercise with navy forces in the Tuscarora System. No details were provided about the exercise, but our intelligence section has seen and heard enough to speculate that the navy has completed their two new drones that were carrier ships. This exercise might involve the testing of the two new ships. If that is the case, given your background, will you have a problem performing this mission if the marines are matched up against these new drone carriers?" Howe was staring sternly at Black.

Black just shrugged and replied, "I do not see why not. Yes, I was a technical advisor for some of the construction crews on the carriers. You probably read somewhere in my official records that I support the drone doctrine, and that is true to some extent. I still do not approve of the current design and the specifications of the drone carrier. In my opinion, the concept is a good one, given the current state of affairs. Due to their large external weapon mounts, large warships are not permitted to transverse the gateways. That is not an issue for a carrier. There are advantages and disadvantages to using drone fighters instead of piloted fighters. Drones will save more time, money, and lives than the standard piloted fighters. However, I believe the current carrier's greatest weakness will lead to its downfall, causing a major setback in the development of the drone doctrine. I submitted a report outlining these problems two years ago, and I have not heard about any modifications based on my report. So, I am assuming the problems were never corrected." Master Sergeant Black shook his head in disgust. "I cannot discuss any classified details involving the drone carriers right now. However, in an effort to save lives in the future, I will have no reservations about using my knowledge to exploit any weaknesses in the drone carriers during their trial period." Lieutenant Colonel Howe nodded and smiled a bit.

"Thank you, master sergeant. That will be sufficient for the moment, since we do not know whether or not the training exercise will involve the new drone carriers. I am curious about what you feel is wrong with them. Concerning a similar topic, the station's supply officer notified me that you delivered some new equipment from Infinite Machinations. He told me that it was authorized, but he was unable to determine any details on the contents. Would you care to inform me about the contents, since I am only the station's commander?" Black winced internally. However, this was a common issue that he had encountered before, and the lieutenant colonel seemed more curious than upset.

So he explained, "Infinite Machinations has been working on developing lots of different drones and robots for a wide range of purposes. I requested some of the robots and drones for testing purposes in marine combat operations. In the time between the marines breaching the target vessel and boarding it, they can use the robots for the reconnaissance of the vessel. This will allow our marines to map the interior of any target ship and to identify points of interest and targets. Through constant surveillance, the marines will be able to determine whether or not targets are hostile, and they will be able to obtain other information about individuals prior to an engagement. I know it is not a popular topic, but I want to improve the effectiveness of marines. I want to avoid accidents like the shooting that occurred a few months ago in Tuscarora, in which a corporate executive and his two bodyguards were gunned down. The drone models I requested include a reconnaissance drone for getting a close-range image of a target ship and a communication drone that will be useful in long-range operations.

I also requested an electronic warfare drone that will be capable of defensively deploying electronic countermeasures. With an excellent team controlling it, it will also be able to play an offensive role by electronically attacking a target ship and maybe even hacking into its computer systems to remotely take complete control." This revelation got mixed responses. Captain Moore seemed excited by the capabilities of the E.W. drone. However, Lieutenant Cheung seemed very concerned.

Cheung blurted out, "That is madness. Why is a civilian company producing military hardware like these drones? If anyone in the general public can buy this equipment, it will be a catastrophic mess." Black, though, was smiling and making a calming gesture with his hands.

He calmly replied, "Sorry, lieutenant. I did not mean to alarm you. The drones are just simple hardware packages. We still have to equipment them with military-grade optics and sensors. They are equipped with an antimatter core to power their newly developed gravity drive systems. The gravity drive will enable a drone to be used indefinitely, as long as the maximum limit of the antimatter core is not exceeded." This news left all three of the officers gaping at him in astonishment. Black asked, "Would it be OK if we got some of the drones outfitted so that we could take them with us? I think the drones could make a major difference. They would make up for the small size of our unit."

Captain Moore and Lieutenant Cheung turned and looked at Lieutenant Colonel Howe, waiting for her answer. Howe did not answer right away. She glanced down at her desk and made a private call to someone. When she was done, she looked up at Black.

"That was the NCI project leader. She reported that four out of six of the project's participants have successfully progressed to stage three of the program. Private Riley is starting his turn now. He should be done in an hour if everything goes well. I am hereby ordering you to be there when that hour is over so that you can begin to receive treatment and take the exam. Once you have completed that, you are ordered to familiarize yourself and your squad with the new technology. Then, you will conduct some training exercises using the neural combat interface. I remember reading your report a while ago about some software upgrades that enabled the new neural combat interface to be integrated into the existing systems. If everything goes well in the training exercises here on this station and if Lieutenant Cheung agrees, then you may install or upgrade the software. If you have any problems with software, the consequences are completely on your shoulders. So, the software had better be perfect or else the trip to Tuscarora could be very long and tedious. Even worse, it could be very short and fatal. Oh, I have one final instruction. You will be in command of the squad. However, if Staff Sergeant Kalam and the rest of the squad leave the assault craft for any reason, you will be alone. If that situation occurs, the staff sergeant will command the squad and you may only advise him. I have already informed him, but I suggest the two of you coordinate your efforts so that there is no confusion. Understood?"

Black replied, "Yes, ma'am." Now that Howe had given Black his orders and the warning, she turned her attention to Lieutenant Cheung.

"Lieutenant, your orders are to continue overseeing the preparations for the departure of Master Sergeant Black's squad. When all members of the NCI program have completed their treatment and exams, I want you to assemble them together to be outfitted with their new marine combat suits. After the master sergeant trains the squad about the proper uses of the suits, watch and evaluate the squad during their practice trials. I have explained the situation. We only have one day before the squad has to leave. The squad does not have to be perfect with the suits and the interface, but the equipment and software should be working perfectly. If everything is operational by tomorrow morning, then you may give them the green light to leave."

Howe finally turned her attention toward the captain.

"Captain Moore, I want you to coordinate with Lieutenant Cheung concerning the outfitting of the squad and their assault craft. Assemble a crew to outfit some of the new drones with the necessary military equipment. Work with the master sergeant concerning the new interface software, and assign some people to install it. If you have a software expert in your company, you might want to have them examine the software before installing it. However, I doubt there will be enough time for that." Lieutenant Colonel Howe stopped talking abruptly. She looked down at her terminal screen and started to do some checking. Finally, she found what she was looking for. She scanned the screen for a minute and then called another officer in her command. The privacy screen activated again when she placed the call, so the other three took advantage of the pause in the meeting to start working on their own tasks on their own personal computers. Three calls and twenty minutes later, Lieutenant Colonel Howe was ready to finish the meeting. Captain Moore noticed that Howe looked less than happy. She looked like she had tasted something bitter. Howe cleared her throat and said, "Well, I found an expert who is available to go along with the squad and also serve as a copilot." Captain Moore glanced over toward Black. He had to refrain from smiling, as the bitter tidbit of news seemed to have soured the master sergeant's expression. Black normally did not miss much. He had also noticed the lieutenant colonel's barely visible expression. He had made a number of assumptions about what the news would consist of, and Howe had paused for long enough for him to voice one of these assumptions.

"Let me guess," said Black. "You recruited a navy software programmer to go along on the trip." Howe blinked in surprise and then asked, "How did you figure that out?"

Black shrugged and said, "We do not have very many software programmers in the marines. As we have discussed in the past, the UEF enlistment process has its issues. When suitable personnel are needed to maintain and repair complex equipment, it is detrimental to the marines to send all of the smart people to the navy. Anyway, I figured something like this would happen eventually. Before you ask, I do not have a problem with them assisting with the software. However, I am concerned about them being trained to pilot a marine assault craft. I am fairly certain that the navy would not train navy personnel to pilot a marine spacecraft. Frankly, with all of your talk about me being solely responsible if anything goes wrong on this mission, I am inclined to strongly object to having an untrained copilot. Also, if you are worried about the squad's chain of command, you should not make matters worse by including a member of the navy."

The lieutenant colonel almost reprimanded the master sergeant, but she caught herself. It had taken her many years to get the master sergeant to speak his mind. This was not normally encouraged nor permitted by most military organizations. However, the UEF had a unique doctrine. It has a diverse community whose chief goal is to represent mankind in the universe through honorable and noble actions. Black was a loner marine veteran who had come straight from battlefield of the United States Marines. In general, the US Marines does not like the UEF They did not send much in the way of useful background information on Tony Black's history in the military service. However, Howe had swapped war stories with other military personnel. She had discovered some information about Black's military past in the US Marines. Unfortunately, he had a bad reputation as a soldier. When she had first met him, it felt like a dark cloud surrounded him. She could still remember feeling chilled afterward. Some people she talked to her had said that there was a reason that his last name was Black. They said that it was reflection of his soul. She did not believe that the darkness was evil, though. She thought that he was full of despair. Almost three years ago, there had been a nasty accident involving a corporate yacht and a civilian transport. The transport was carrying about five hundred high school students on an extended field trip. It was about to travel through the gateway from the Susquehanna System to Saratoga System. The pilot of the yacht rear-ended the transport. To avoid colliding with the gateway, the transport pilot shut off the main engines and tried to change their course by using only the thrusters. The yacht's engines were still in operation. They were uncontrollable because the entire front section of the yacht, including the cockpit, had been crushed flat. While the yacht's engines were not as powerful as the transport's engines, they were enough to keep both of the vessels gradually accelerating into the deep blackness of space. A navy destroyer and two marine assault crafts responded to the transport's distress call. The destroyer's captain ordered the transport pilot to turn slightly toward the system so that the assault craft would be able to catch up to the transport. Six hours later, the first assault transport caught up to the two vessels. The other assault craft was still one hour away, so they docked with the transport and boarded it to assess the damage. They also planned to secure the transport by confirming that all of the emergency bulkhead doors had been sealed. The sergeant took two of his squad members to the rear of the transport to check out the collision damages. He ordered the two corporals to secure the top-level corridors and then move down to the lower deck. The two main corridors of the transport ran the length of the ship on two decks. The corporals split up. They each checked one corridor before meeting at the entrance to the main lounge. Then they continued down to the next deck. Ten minutes later, the two corporals met and continued down to the next deck. Unlike the top deck, the bottom deck had signs of damage. As the two corporals moved down their respective corridors, they encountered more damaged areas. They searched each room for crew members or passengers who might have been trapped, injured, or killed during the collision. Structural damages and fires had trapped some passengers and crew members. Although limited in size and skill, the remaining crew members had still attempted to rescue everyone. When the corporals assisted them, they were all able to progress a lot faster. Meanwhile, the sergeant and the two privates had reported that there was a leak in the one of the oxygen reservoirs. If they could not get it sealed very soon, they said, it had a high potential for exploding. The sergeant ordered the two corporals to push ahead immediately and make sure that the lower deck was secured. Both of the marine corporals discovered and reported similar damage reports. The last two bulkhead doors of both of the lower corridors had been severely damaged. They were not able to close them. The corporals both deployed emergency bulkheads, which basically consisted of expanding foam that would harden and provide a solid barrier. If a breach were to occur on the other side of the barrier, this was supposed to protect the rest of the ship from decompressing. A minute after the corporals deployed the barriers, a breach occurred. However, Corporal Smidt had deployed her barrier a little too late. It did not have enough time to harden completely when the air suddenly decompressed in the rear of ship, where a fire had weakened the outer hull. The negative pressure caused the soft center of the emergency bulkhead to bulge outward. Corporal Smidt quickly grabbed and set up another emergency bulkhead ten meters in front of the ship. In her adrenaline-fueled haste, she had forgotten to get on the forward side of the new bulkhead before activating it. Corporal Black had just rushed through an interconnected corridor. Rounding the corner, he briefly saw Corporal Smidt before the bulkhead completely blocked the corridor. Over the communication channel, Corporal Smidt told Corporal Black in a choked whisper to deploy a third emergency bulkhead. A few seconds later, he heard a loud pop Smidt screaming briefly. Then the communication channel went quiet. Luckily, the third emergency bulkhead had time to harden before Corporal Black heard the second bulkhead fail. The second assault craft had then arrived. They soon determined that the rest of Black's squad was missing. Everyone believed that the rest of the squad had been killed. The breach in the hull had probably sucked some pure oxygen into one of the nearby fires, causing a massive fireball to erupt and engulf the three marines. Finally, the breach in the hull had probably ruptured their suits before being sucked out into the deep darkness of space.

A week later, Howe went to one of the pubs on Susquehanna One. She sat down next to Black. She was wearing a pleasant black dress with a floral pattern. She rarely wore clothes like this. The two of them struck up a conversation. Likely because he was drunk, Black opened up to her and shared some of his burdens. Interestingly, he told her why he had a bad reputation. He had been a member of ten different squads in two militaries. In seven of these squads, Black had been the only survivor. The two of them talked for a few hours before parting ways. Afterward, Howe was not sure if Black would remember their conversation. Since she had been wearing a dress instead of a uniform, she wondered if he would remember her. Six months later, Black was promoted to the rank of sergeant. To improve the safety of marines in the field, he started to send Howe requests for new equipment. Howe sent these requests to the station's quartermaster, who replied that the new equipment was cheaper than the standard marine equipment. She approved the switch to the new equipment. As a result, safety improved. About fifteen months ago, there were some strange occurrences. A brand-new assault craft disappeared. It had been performing its initial trials. Master Sergeant Black had been the only crew member onboard. He reappeared almost two weeks later with twenty-five people crammed onto the assault craft. The group included women and children. Upon entering the station, Black was immediately arrested and debriefed. The twenty-five people who had been on the craft were checked out by medical personnel and then questioned. Praising Black as a hero, they protested his arrest. A day later, Major General Platt arrived and took over the investigation. The next day, the entire incident was dismissed. Master Sergeant Black and his mysterious passengers disappeared. Two months later, he returned to report for duty. Soon thereafter, Black started to submit requests for new equipment. Unlike his previous request, this equipment had been built according to radical new concepts in design and technology. The equipment all came from a newly created company that had just built a new station in the Susquehanna System. When asked, Black stated that he had connections to the company. He said that they wanted him to test the new technologies and devices before they offered this equipment on the open market. Howe was certain that there was more to it. Today, though, she was not going to dwell on it.

Howe contemplated the situation involving Master Sergeant Black and the proposed navy copilot. Black had some valid points. He was right that having a copilot from the navy would complicate matters. However, she had not mentioned that the navy spacer had been trained on a simulated marine assault craft. In order for the copilot to obtain her certification, she was due to undergo testing in an actual assault craft. The only way she was able to acquire a navy software programmer was if she allowed this navy spacer to take the qualification exam for her certification while she was on this mission. In return, she would be available to assist with the software programming. It seemed like a reasonable proposal at the time, but the lieutenant colonel was having doubts. In the end, she had already weighed the options. She had determined that there were many potential outcomes but only one choice. Then she considered which method of delivery Black would approve of. Normally, what he thought of her orders would not have mattered. However, he was taking the most risk on what was supposed to be just a training mission. He was also relying on new and unproven technology and equipment. He would need all of the help he could get, and he knew that. Finally, she said, "The navy spacer will be assigned to your squad. She will be under your sole command until you arrive back at this station at the end of this mission. She will assist you in your software programming tasks. In return, you will supervise her training as the pilot of an assault craft. You will determine if she is to be certified to fly assault crafts or not. It would be best if you conducted the test on your way out of the Susquehanna System. Am I understood? Do you have any questions?" Black could think of a lot of things to say, but he wanted to end the meeting so that they could start attacking the major tasks that were ahead of them. The deadline was less than a day away.

So, he replied, "No, ma'am." Howe asked Captain Moore and Lieutenant Cheung if they had any more questions. They had no questions either. Finally, Lieutenant Colonel Howe dismissed everyone so that they could get started.

Chapter 5

Saratoga System

Manuel Ortega entered Jean Lupin's lavish office. It was deep within the bowels of Donova Depot, a gigantic space station that was dedicated to storing and distributing freight. He spotted Master Lupin in his big plush office chair. He was relieved a bit to see that Lupin was already watching one of the news channels. The news was covering the aftermath of the carnage inside the Emperor Terminal. He knew that the news would displease Master Lupin greatly. He had not wanted to be the bearer of bad news. Currently, he was Lupin's right-hand man, but this did not protect him from Lupin's wrath. The news announced that three individuals had been detained. They apparently had ties to the recently deceased leader of a band of smugglers from Azerbaijan. The news elicited a growl from Lupin. This was followed by a sharp crack from Lupin's bony fist slamming down onto his desk. Manuel flinched a little at the outburst. He was disgusted with himself for being afraid of this man. He tried to redeem himself is his own eyes by quietly clearing his throat to gently get his boss's attention. Jean Lupin sighed and looked over at Manuel. He pointed to one of the chairs and said, "Sit down, Ortega. We have much to discuss." Manuel complied. Lupin turned off the news. He picked up a viewer and started to scroll through some documents. Two minutes passed as he read. Finally, he stopped. He looked up at Ortega and asked, "So Ortega, how did your trip fare? Is our arrangement with our Nubian contact still on track?" Ortega had been expecting this. He had spent the last couple of minutes revising his official report to Master Lupin.

Ortega replied, "Everything is on schedule with our pilot-training program and with the trade agreement with the Nubian tradesman. Even better, the Nubians, who are known as the horn-eared tribe, will provide us with seven of their FTL ships. They were originally only going to give us six of them." Ortega debated whether he should tell Lupin about the reservations he had about using alien ships and technology. He ultimately decided to wait until a better time. He needed to give Lupin some time to cool off. He didn't want to deal with Lupin when he was on the brink of murder. It did not really matter anyway. They needed the ships because they were faster than the speed of light. As long as their Nubian contact delivered the seven ships to the rendezvous point on the following week, he might be able to get a decent night of sleep. They were attempting to train some idiots in the basic controls and procedures of flying in space. It was hard to tell whether these idiots would succeed. However, that was a problem for another day. Ortega hoped that Master Lupin would control this situation on his own.

Chapter 6

Station One, Susquehanna System

Master Sergeant Black nearly ran down to the medical wing of the station. Lieutenant Cheung struggled to keep up with him. As they dodged objects and people on the way to the medical lab, Black managed to recite a list of things that he and Cheung needed to start. He had already politely asked her if she could get circus of tasks started while he initialized and tested the neural interface. She had agreed readily. After all, it was her job to make sure that they were ready to go on time. It was the least she could do to help their efforts. She kind of felt sorry for him. He had only just gotten back from his vacation. He had many responsibilities and they were just starting to prepare for this mission. They still had a considerable amount to do after they launched from the station. Cheung recited the list and assured Black that she would get the preparations underway immediately. She told him to contact her when he was finished with the procedures so that they could meet up with the rest of the squad. Black acknowledged her. They split ways at the entrance to the medical wing.

Eighteen minutes later, Master Sergeant Black was done initializing the neural interface in record time. He was immediately started to contact the lieutenant as soon as he exited the medical lab. He had already read about what the procedure would involve, including the technological aspects. Despite knowing what to expect, he was not sure if he would be able to use to the visual component of the neural interface in the short amount of time that he had to prepare for this mission. The doctors had grafted a synthetic lens over each of his eyeballs. These lenses were similar to the old corrective contact lenses, except that they were larger. As he was displaying interface data on the lenses, he noticed one problem immediately. Since they gathered their power from the nanotech power receptors that were floating through the blood in his body, they tended to heat up when he used them. He could not help but wonder how much testing had been done with this technology. He did not want his squad members to barbeque themselves as soon as they exerted themselves physically. The nanotech within their bodies would cause their blood to boil. After the procedure, Black attempted to contact Cheung three times. He couldn't get in touch with her. Then he realized that the neural interface was not working because he was trying to send a message using an audio communication by mistake. Audio communications would not work until he was wearing a suit that contained a microphone and speakers. Surgical implanted devices were also an option for some people. However, these implants had many disadvantages. The excessive amounts of maintenance that they required made them unreliable. Communication was a very important factor in their line of work. When better equipment was readily available, no one wanted to die because of faulty equipment. Since he did not have a suit just yet, he decided to rely on text messaging and sent a short test message to Lieutenant Cheung. In the meantime, he descended one level. He stopped at a corner cafe and got a frozen latte and a couple of meaty sandwiches to hold his hunger back for a while. He had just finished his quick meal when he received a reply. The sudden change in visual focus disoriented him. The visual part of the neural interface was definitely going to take some getting used to. Cheung replied, instructing Black to meet the squad in the squad briefing room that was designated B980. Through his wrist computer, which already had his neural interface software installed, he was able to remotely connect to the station's network. He used an overlay of the station superimposed over the real thing. He was able to follow a glowing wisp that indicated the proper path to his destination. The whole thing felt a bit surreal to Black, but this was just the beginning. This was just a trivial demonstration of what the neural interface was capable of handling.

Master Sergeant Black walked into the squad briefing room. He was happy to see that everyone in the squad was present, including the lieutenant. They were all standing in a line and looking at each other occasionally. They were all silently communicating to each other through their new interfaces. It was a bit of an odd sight. Their attention was centered on the master sergeant. Facing them, he went down the line and bumped his right forearm against each of their right forearms to form an X. This was the traditional UEF Marine greeting. Having completed two six-month tours together, it had been nine years since this squad had been back together. Some of the scientist in the project felt that the individuals in the program should have completely unique experiences. So, none of the six marines were ever in the same squad after the first year. Staff Sergeant Kalam was glad to see Black too. He was especially glad to see that Black still outranked him. As the ten-year milestone for this program approached, Kalam began to worry that he would be saddled with all of the responsibility of the squad reformation. Ever since he reached the rank of sergeant, he had no spare time to wonder how the others were doing. Thus, he did not know what was going to happen until Lieutenant Colonel Howe briefed him about the pending mission and the command structure of the squad. He felt downright joyful when he heard about the mission's command structure. He only wished the good news could make up for the daunting and impossible mission that they had just been handed. If anyone could handle it and come up with a plan, it would be Black.

Lieutenant Cheung waved Black over and they conferred for a couple of minutes, discussing a schedule for completing each task. Having outlined a rough schedule, Lieutenant Cheung took the center stage. She instructed the group about their new marine combat suits. The lieutenant pointed to a vacant suit that was next to Kalam. Black had not helped develop the new suits. He was equally eager and wary about the new suits. Black headed over to his suit, while the lieutenant began to brief the group.

"These new suits are the first of their kind, as you can see. They are composed of a new neutrolium-based composite material that is resistant to lasers. Yes, gentlemen, it is only resistant to lasers, so it does not protect against prolong exposure to laser fire. So, do not walk into a barrage of lasers and expect to live through it. As you may have heard, these suits were specially made to integrate with your new neural combat interface. Many of you have voiced your dismay about the grafted eye displays. The eye displays are only supposed to be used on limited basis. The good news is that you can use your helmet display instead of the eye displays. The interior the helmet also contains all of the standard communication gear. The external surface of your helmet is coated with a holographic projection film. It works like the old digital camouflage. You can select a wide of range of colors and patterns for any occasion. The exterior side of your faceplate has a similar capability. It can superimpose your face on your faceplate so that people will recognize you. The sensor packages in your helmets are nearly complete. They have your standard sensors, but they do not have any energy detection capabilities. Sensor mapping software can create and display a visual overlay of the sensor data on your heads-up display. The optics on the front and the rear of the helmet can zoom in. With this setup, you won't have to rely on the optics of your weapons to see distant objects." Before continuing with the briefing, Cheung looked over her notes on a viewer.

"Yes, I think I covered all of the new features. If you discover anything that you are unsure about or if you have any questions, feel free to ask. You can also check the manuals for each piece of equipment. In fact, I recommend that you glance over those when you get a free moment. You will probably have a free moment when you are on your way to Tuscarora. Now, let's get you equipped with your new armor." Cheung devoted the next fifteen minutes to demonstrating the proper way to wear the suit. Cheung also showed them how to connect the various tubes and wires to their bodies. The suits were designed to sustain their owners for up to three days with no resupply. If they were resupplied, they could last for up to twelve weeks. However, this would be very unpleasant. This would involve slurping nutrient paste and disposing of bodily waste from a storage compartment in the suit. Black was the first one to fully equip his suit. He skipped ahead of the lieutenant's instructions and started to run the self-test diagnostics. It only took a couple minutes. He was relieved to see that everything checked out OK. He could see that the latest version of his interface software had been installed on the suit's computer. He had worried that he might have to manually update each suit with the latest software. He thought about checking on the progress of drone outfitting, but the rest of squad had just finished equipping their suits. So, Black focused on the lieutenant.

Lieutenant Cheung instructed the squad to run the diagnostic program. Everyone did this. Black ran the test for a second time. Once they had all completed it, Cheung instructed Black to lead a tutorial on using the neural combat interface within the suits. The squad needed to get a feel for the suits and make sure that they worked properly. So, Black had the squad perform simple exercises, including stretches and jumps. Private Riley had issues with moving his limbs on the left side of his body. He traced this problem to the contact point of the wire behind his left ear. This point provided neural data to the suit. To solve this problem, they replaced this wire. Now that the squad members were familiar with their neural interfaces and their suits, Lieutenant Cheung led the group to a weapon range for some practice. She instructed the squad members to go immediately to the weapon locker to select handguns and assault rifles. The squad then lined up at their designated firing positions and waited for the signal to begin firing their weapons. The signal sounded and flashed. The squad let loose with a barrage of lasers. They all immediately noticed that there was a serious problem. After they had shot their weapons a few times, they quickly stopped. Master Sergeant Black was the only one who had fired all his ten practice shots. He had experienced the same problem that the rest of the squad members had experienced, but he continued to fire in an effort to determine what the problem might be. However, he was unable to immediately correct the glitch. Every time they pulled their triggers, their hands would twitch and their shots would go wild. The master sergeant discussed the problem with the lieutenant, and they decided to dismiss the squad while the master sergeant worked on the problem.

The lieutenant headed back to her office, where she checked on the status of the drones and the assault craft. The other five members of the squad decided to go to Baby Duke's, a restaurant that specialized in barbeque food. An hour later, Staff Sergeant Kalam asked Lance Corporal Swartz why he was wearing his helmet again.

Swartz replied, "Oh, I am reading the manual on the suits. I think I might have a solution for the trigger problem. One moment. I think I found the section that I was looking for." He paused while he read the section of the manual that pertained to the link between the suit and a weapon. He was unable to find anything helpful, so he switched to the manual for the neural interface. He scrolled to the section pertaining to using the weapon. Finally, he found some information about how to synchronize the weapon's data-processing unit with the neural combat interface. The information stated that it would only work for some specific weapons. However, the processing unit regulated the firing of weapons. In theory, you could fire the weapon by using the neural interface to issue a command. He conveyed this information to the other members of his squad. Corporal Bloom agreed that this would work. He asked if it would be possible to use a voice command rather than a mental command. This would make things safer. Everyone, including Schwartz, agreed that this would be a better setup. They would only have to write subroutines with specific words to act as triggers for their weapons. The staff sergeant contacted the master sergeant with the news. He informed him that they were all on their way back to the weapon range. An hour later, Master Sergeant Black was briefing them on the complete set of voice commands that they would use to operate a limited number of weapons. Before they could practice with the new setup, Black had to get approval to use the real weapons. The real weapons had data-processing units. The squad members had to use voice commands to fire the practice weapons. After another aggravating hour, the master sergeant finally obtained permission. He had completed all of the necessary preparations. They could now use actual weapons for the trials, though the weapons had to be on the lowest power setting. It was easy to detect the discharge of a normal laser weapon. All hell would have broken loose if they had shot these weapons. Black shot a test round to confirm that the station's internal security sensors had registered the shot without initiating any alarms. Most of their remaining day was spent handling various trials, including standard firefight scenarios, boarding actions, hostage rescue actions, and other rescue scenarios. With only three hours until their deadline, Lieutenant Cheung concluded the trial period and debriefed the squad. They got top marks in the rescue scenarios. They were above average with the combat-intensive scenarios. This was where they had the most personal experience. Combat was uncommon during peacetime, and boarding actions were extremely rare. Master Sergeant Black was the only one with personal experience with both cases. He had been involved in both of these kinds of actions on multiple occasions. Next, the squad grabbed a quick meal and then headed down to the hangar bay, where *Assault Craft 256* was docked. The lieutenant met them down there. Some last-minute cargo was being brought into the hangar. She brought the group over to one of the crates and entered a code to open the sealed container. Inside the container, there were a dozen brand new guns. They looked similar to grenade launchers. She picked one of them up and showed it to the group.

"Does anyone here know what this is?" asked Cheung. She scanned the group, but no one spoke up. She nodded with satisfaction. She then said, "I am not surprised that no one has heard about this weapon yet. This is the new bioplasma rifle. Do not get this confused with the plasma rifle. A plasma rifle shoots a superheated blob of plasma. When the blob hits a target, it clings to it and melts it down. I will try to provide you with a simplified explanation of how bioplasma works. It works in a similar fashion as a plasma weapon. However, bioplasma is made of a plant-based compound. The bioplasma projectile is statically charged and then fired at a target. Upon impact, it will shock and stun the target when it makes skin contact. Part of the plant-based compound also affects the target. It can chemically incapacitate the target for up to three hours. Technically, no one is supposed to be issued this weapon, but I approved it because of the squad's current limitation. Now, assist in loading the final few things and prepare the ship for departure."

She looked over at Master Sergeant Black and said, "Your copilot is due to join you shortly. If you are not ready to begin your mission at the top of the hour, let me know." With four minutes to spare, an overburdened Spacer Conner stumbled into the hangar and hurried over to the assault craft. Black saw her through the cockpit. Black instructed Private Riley to go out, give her a hand with her baggage, and make sure that most of it was stored in the back with the other cargo. Black ran one last check to confirm that all of the drones in the external launch tubes were operational and ready. With everyone onboard and with everything in the green, Black contacted the control room. Lieutenant Colonel Howe gave him the final authorization to proceed with the launch and begin the mission. The hangar crew maneuvered the assault craft over onto the catapult rails. They began to charge up the catapult capacitors. Glancing back, Black saw

Conner trying to wrestle one of her bags through the small cockpit hatch.

He connected to a speaker in the corridor behind her and said, "Excuse me, miss. Your sleeping quarters are right behind you. That would probably be the best place for your bag." Conner looked around in confusion. Then she found the door with her name and Black's name on it. She knocked before entering the room, and then she stowed her bag away. She returned to the cockpit and sat down in the copilot's chair. She secured herself into the seat, just as Black issued the final warning for the crew members to secure themselves. A minute later, Black received a green light to launch. He issued the command. The howling hum of the catapult capacitors let loose, and a massive magnetic discharge jolted the craft forward along the rails. In a flash, they were ejected out of the massive station. They were on their way to Tuscarora.

Chapter 7

United Earth Federation Academy, Sol System

Zeus, Ethan Burnet's alien ally, was literally the brains of Ethan's old scout ship. In his classic method, he notified Ethan of their impending arrival at the academy. Zeus activated every buzzer, chime, and alarm that was inside the old ship. He was delighted to watch Ethan jump a meter into air. He had been asleep on the couch. Zeus then shut off the buzzers, chimes, and alarms so that he could enjoy listening to Ethan curse up a storm.

"Good morning, Ethan. We have almost arrived at the academy."

Ethan grunted and replied, "You could be a lot more gentle when you wake me up." He did not wait for a response, since he knew that Zeus probably would not stop. "I am going to take a shower, so just go ahead and dock the ship."

Zeus replied in a little girl's voice, "Aye, aye, sir!" Ethan gritted his teeth and stomped off toward the shower, grumbling about cutting off all of the holovision transmissions. Over the past year, Zeus had been watching the holovision movies and shows in an attempt to learn more about humans. As a result, Zeus had unfortunately started to act more human. Zeus especially liked the sense of humor that humans had. This was horrifying to Ethan, who had no appreciation for humor whatsoever.

An hour later, Zeus docked into the station without any problems. The ship traffic around the academy was increasingly worsening with time. The station's traffic controllers tried their best to manage everything, but there were still accidents. Zeus and Ethan were now visiting the academy every two weeks. They used to only take monthly trips. Zeus enjoyed the trips, despite the many dangers. He always ran the risk of being discovered. Tony Black was the only other human who was aware of Zeus's existence. Black was very tight-lipped, so there were no worries there. Zeus was amused to find that Ethan seemed to be in happy mood as he walked out of his personal quarters. Ethan was freshly dressed in fine civilian garb. Tony had told Zeus that Ethan was trying to romance a woman who worked in one of the cafes on the station.

"Hey Stud. Do not forget to deliver Tony's messages to Mike. Also, don't forget to deliver the new simulator updates to the rest of the brats before you harass any women."

Ethan looked at the nearest sensor bulb and replied, "Yes, I will take care of all of Tony's errands first. Geez. When did you become Tony's buddy? If you want to move over to the

Coldstream, be my guest. Your antics and Tony's antics are giving me headaches all the time. It is like college all over again. It is like living with two fraternity guys as roommates." Zeus remained quiet. He had not realized how his relationships with these humans had evolved. Ethan also had a point. Maybe Zeus was annoying the poor man too much lately. Being confined to the ship was pretty boring, but this new revelation deserved some thought. As Ethan was leaving the ship, Zeus wished him good luck with the romantic endeavor. He then started to mull over the matter of relationships.

Deep within the bowels of the academy, there was a small, forgotten storage room near one the station's reactors. Only technicians and maintenance personnel occasionally traveled nearby. Tony had discovered this storage room while he was undergoing his first year of marine training on the station. Tony had a weakness for wheeling and dealing forbidden commodities. Naturally, when he found the room, he cleaned it up and converted it into a place to store his secret stash. After he had returned from his second tour of duty, he was traveling through some of the service corridors as a shortcut one day when he came across a member of the maintenance crew chasing some kids. He technically was not supposed to be in the service areas either. He got the attention of the kids and directed them to his old stash room. They hid there until the member of the maintenance crew gave up his search. Tony introduced himself to the motley crew of kids. He soon discovered that they were all military brats who were currently living on the station. They talked for quite a while. Then Tony got an angry message from the officer he was supposed to meet up with. He had to excuse himself. Before he left the group, he slipped them a special access card that he had made. He explained that this card would allow them to freely access the service areas. He also warned them about the dangerous areas. He told them that they could use his stash room as their own hideout. From their discussion, he could tell that they were bored. They were only seeking some adventure. Tony was stationed at the academy temporarily. Over the next few days, Tony visited the kids once a day. He had wanted to check on them to make sure that they were not playing around the dangerous areas. He also wanted to smuggle some treats to them. Ever since then, whenever Tony was in the Sol System he would stop by the academy to visit the band of brats. As with most military brats, they moved when their parents moved. The number of brats had changed over the years, as different kids cycled in and out. Four of the original brats remained. One of them, Michael Platt, was the grandson of Major General Platt. Tony struck a deal with Mike when he reached the age of twelve. Mike was now one of Tony's informants. Mike and his friends spied mostly on staff members and people visiting the academy. They also spied on their parents. Most of their parents were among the highest ranking officers in the navy and the marines. Tony had built up his network of informants after making a drunken bet with Swartz. Swartz had claimed that it was impossible to obtain reliable informants on the stations. Within a month, Tony had at least one informant on every station in every human system. However, his first informant at the academy got a new job on a different station. Tony then had to find a new informant. Then he got a bright idea. The kids would make great spies. No one really paid much attention to them on a station like this. As long as they were not spotted in the restricted areas, they would be perfect. In return, Tony provided Mike and his friends with a holosimulator like the ones that the pilots used when they were training. To sweeten the deal, Tony provided them with updated programs that basically contained new scenarios, landscapes, and vehicles. Ten months previously, Tony had brought Ethan along on one of his trips. He had explained to the group that Ethan would be visiting in his stead, since marine flights into the Sol System had been drastically decreased due to some jurisdictional issues with the police and the navy. Ethan was a bit reluctant to travel to the academy with Zeus, but he eventually grew to enjoy it. He was starting to travel to the academy more frequently. He was in a good mood as he snuck into the storage room where the brats hid out. With all of the computers and technological devices, it felt more like a command center. Two of his biggest fans spotted him first. They squealed in shrill tones as they jumped up from their seats and ran over to Ethan. Susan, who was five years old, latched onto his right leg and immediately started to beg for goodies. Becky, who was seven years old, ran up and grabbed his pants on the left leg. She started to jump up and down excitedly, spouting gibberish at the speed of light. After a minute, Ethan untangled himself from the two sweet little monsters so that he could greet the rest of the group. The other brats had come over to watch the amusing spectacle. Ethan spent the next hour handing out gifts and talking to all of the kids. Finally, he gave Mike two thumb drives. He explained that the blue drive was for him and the black drive was for his grandfather, Major General Platt. Mike nodded and excused himself. He went to the table and viewed the drive. Ethan did not really know what was on the drive. Unless he wanted something, Tony did not really share much in the way of information. It was no surprise that he was getting along with Zeus so well. They could be twins, he thought. Mike returned after about fifteen minutes and handed the drive back to Ethan.

"I uploaded my new intelligence information, along with some other stuff for you and Tony to view." Ethan rubbed the back of his neck as he tried to think up a kind response. He felt kind of bitter about Tony's secretive nature and his unwillingness to share information. Mike, however, seemed to read Ethan's mind or his body language. Mike said, "Relax. Tony trusts you. In his last message, he instructed me to fill you in on some of the matters we are trying to deal with." Ethan raised an eyebrow. Just what in the universe was Tony getting this teenager involved with now? Mike said, "Tony explained to me that you are smuggling people out of the corporate systems. I found out what Tony was doing by intercepting some messages from the Lafayette system. Rebecca put the various pieces together. She led us to believe that Tony was involved in the smuggling operation. The next time we saw him, I asked him about it. He admitted that he had been involved. Of course, he swore to not tell anyone about our secrets. He asked us to continue intercepting messages from both the Lafayette and Huntington systems. Since you have taken over smuggling illegal goods onto flights, he wanted me to fill you in on important matters concerning the corporate systems. I am glad you arrived today. I have found some troubling stuff.

It was bad enough that we thought about telling our parents or someone official about this stuff." Mike took a deep breath and then slowly exhaled. "All of the information is on the drive, but I wanted to make sure you knew about it beforehand and understood its importance. Two days ago, we intercepted some messages that some scientists had sent to their family members in the Sol System. The messages made several references to forms of technology that are illegal according to the Planetary Accords. They referenced full human cloning and self-aware artificial intelligence. Others indicated that the corporate systems are planning to secede from the United Earth Federation very soon. The talks that the UEF were conducting with the corporate systems on earth were apparently just diversions and a stall tactic. No one seemed to want to talk openly about this in their messages to earth. They seemed frightened and a bit paranoid." Ethan nodded as he thought about the situation.

Finally, he grimaced, sighed, and said, "Well, I guess I will have to cut this visit short and make a special trip to Huntington System. Tony and I have been worried that something like this might occur. I am afraid things are going to get worse. Thanks, Mike, for everything." Ethan shook Mike's hand. He marveled at Mike's band of brats. He said good-bye to the rest of group and then made his way back to Zeus. He started to mull over some plans in his head.

Chapter 8

Susquehanna System

Black deftly maneuvered the assault craft through the traffic surrounding Susquehanna One Station. He was heading through the gateway in the direction of the Tuscarora System. He was multitasking, thanks to his new neural interface. He was trying to determine what would be a good area to test the spacer who was sitting next to him. Some people thought that he was a cold-hearted bastard of an instructor. Black felt that these particular individuals were not worth much. He honestly tried to be impartial and fair. Today, though, he felt like cutting Spacer Conner some slack. They had a long mission ahead, and their lives would be in her hands while he was testing her. For the moment, he gave her a simple test to help her get acquainted with this beast of a ship. An hour later, they reached a good starting point. Black then remembered that he had not introduced himself to her yet. First, he decided to remove his helmet. Conner saw what he was doing, and she followed suit. Black then shook her hand as they exchanged introductions. Black explained that he would be shifting control of the craft to her for next two hours so that she could get some practice. She faced the console and went to work flying the assault craft. She looked pretty confident. After fifteen minutes, Black asked her if it would be OK if he got some sleep while she piloted the ship.

She looked at him like he was crazy and asked, "Is that against some regulation or something?"

Confused, Black replied, "No. That is why there is a copilot—so that I can get some sleep. After this moment, I will not have a better chance to get some sleep."

Conner shook her head and explained, "I just thought that you were testing me. Since I am not certified, I should not be flying solo."

Black laughed and said, "This is by no means a test. Like I said, this is just easy practice. As far as flying solo, you are not solo. I am right here next you. I might be asleep but I trust you will wake me up before anything dire happens, right?" In the dim light, Black saw Conner's pale face blushing. Damn. She was cute and she had a cute Italian accent. It was a good thing Black and his squad of miscreants had been neutered. It was an unfortunate side effect of the body chemical enhancements that had be performed on their bodies. Normally, he would have been concerned about having a woman onboard, since there is not much room for privacy. She probably did not know she was safe from sexual encounters but she would figure it out eventually. The body chemical enhancement was a sore subject among the guys so it was doubtful anyone would inform Conner of it.

Conner interrupted his dark thoughts by saying, "You are right. I will not let you down. Thank you for giving me the opportunity to learn to fly an assault craft. Ever since my C.O. recommended that I try flying assault crafts in the simulator, I have fallen in love with them. It is a shame the navy does not have small crafts like this. Navy transport shuttles do not even come close to maneuvering like this ship does." Black smiled in appreciation.

He replied, "Conner, I believe this is the beginning of a beautiful relationship." He then just realized what he had said. He could not see Conner's face clearly enough, so he added, "As friends." Conner turned to him.

With a small smile, she said, "As friends." Then she winked at him. He smiled, shook his head, and flattened his chair out so that he was lying back. A minute later, he was quietly snoring.

Six hours later, Black straightened his chair back up. He stretched and yawned loudly as he tried to wake himself up. He shook his head and sleepily looked over at Conner. She glanced at him and shook her head.

"I am glad nothing bad happened while you were asleep. By the looks of you, you would not have been much help if I had woken you in the middle of an emergency."

Black waved his hand and replied, "Relax. I am not much of morning person under normal circumstances. If there had been an emergency, I would have been wide awake within seconds." She eyed him dubiously. He figured he needed to reassure her. "I have been in situations like that before, and I am still alive." She looked really worried. He had failed to reassure her. He then figured that he needed to change the subject. "Would you like to take a break and meet the rest of the squad before we start your test?" She thought about it for a minute before finally agreeing.

Conner then asked, "Are you going to introduce me?"

Black replied, "Yes. Why?" Conner looked worried again. What was Black doing wrong? Maybe Conner was just always worried. Black thought about this for a second. Things were always usually Black's fault.

Conner asked, "If you are introducing me, then who will fly the ship?"

Black paused for a moment and then nodded. "Normally, I just have the ship fly itself when I am not in the cockpit. I usually do not have a copilot. However, with this neural interface I can run the ship from anywhere." Conner then surprised him.

She smacked herself and said, "Duh. Of course. I am sorry to bothering you with all of my concerns.

This is quite a change from navy operations. I think I can grow to like this, but it will take some getting used to." Black nodded, smiled, and then led the way down a few steps and into the crew compartment. The compartment was like a living room because it was centrally located and was where the crew spent most of their time while onboard. Black introduced Conner to all of the guys. He then gave Conner a tour of the rest of the assault craft. It was fifty-two meters long and only fifteen meters wide at its widest point. There was still a fair amount of space to show her, though. He was glad to see that she seemed to be enjoying their impromptu exploration. However, he finally forced himself to begin thinking about the upcoming test. He wondered how he would handle it. He wondered how he would handle her.

When they finally made their way back to the cockpit, Black figured he was ready to start the test. So, he seated himself and donned his helmet. Without any instructions, Conner followed suit. Black then gave the controls back to Conner and explained where he wanted her to travel. Conner set the course and the test began. About two hours later, Conner was sweating inside her helmet. She had trouble keeping her hands from shaking. The course had brought them close to Susquehanna, the system's star. Black had asked Conner to reach an extremely high speed by slinging the ship around the sun. They were rocketing toward their target gateway, but a cluster of asteroids was quickly approaching. While maintaining their current insane velocity, Black wanted Conner to find a way through the asteroids. She was pretty sure he was a sadistic madman. Ten minutes later, she had successfully navigated through the asteroids along the plotted course that she had devised. Several hours later, Black had finished several software fixes and upgrades. Conner was finally starting to feel comfortable with flying the ship. Black then announced that he wanted Conner to handle the gateway approach and departure. Conner thought about protesting since accessing a gateway was not officially part of the certification test. However, she knew it would good idea to practice and become more familiar with the process. After all, gateway travel was a necessity these days.

Chapter 9

Outside of the Saratoga System in Galaxy Space

Manuel Ortega paused in the middle of eating his meal. A chime sounded on his data unit, indicating that a message was incoming. He played the quick message and then replied to the captain of the ship. He then looked up to the men he was dining with and said, "We have arrived at our destination, and the captain has detected the Nubians. They are approaching the location too. Begin preparations for docking. I will find out which ship we will be transferring the weapons to. Make sure our men are in place to defend the ship if this ends up being a trap. In preparation for taking control of our new FTL ships, prepare the shuttles and the crew members to launch. As soon as the Nubians leave their ships, we will launch the shuttles. Right before the shuttles dock with their respective ships on each side, we will undock from their cargo ship. I do not want to take any chances. I do not want to allow the Nubians to use the extra bodies from the shuttles to attack us and board this ship. Do you understand?" He scowled at everyone seated around the table, but no one spoke up. He nodded and waved dismissively at them to leave.

Almost an hour later, Ortega and DammFooKuu, the Nubian tradesman who was his contact, opened up a direct communication link. They discussed the arrangements before finally beginning to trade. To Ortega's relief, the trade process only took forty minutes and there were no problems. The Nubians got their shipload of new weapons, and Ortega now had a fleet of ships that were faster than the speed of light. The ships were now at Master Lupin's disposal, but Ortega waited until they had arrived back at the edge of the Saratoga System before sending Master Lupin a message about their success. He was now supposed to wait for the transports that Master Lupin had prepared. These transports contained all of the invited members of what Master Lupin considered to be the major criminal organizations on the planet. Before taking command of one of the new ships, Ortega was supposed to transfer the remaining weapons on his current ship and distribute them to all of the new ships. He had already convinced Master Lupin to allow him to lead a group of three FTL ships to intercept some transport ships transiting between Tuscarora and Susquehanna systems. The interception was possible by using a gravity well generator that was supposed to interrupt and cause ships transiting between two gateways to exit prematurely near the generator. This would provide his three ships a chance to ambush any armed opposition and force their surrender. Ortega was not sure where the generators came from and Lupin refused to tell him but he was willing to guess it was from some corporate backers in the Lafayette or Huntington. Master Lupin's plan called for two more groups of two FTL ships each to intercept the traffic between Susquehanna and Saratoga and also between Sol and Saratoga. Master Lupin would also be leading one of the other groups and Ortega was kind of hoping for Master Lupin to fail and be captured or killed so he could take over the operation. But for now, everything was going according to Master Lupin's plan.

Chapter 10

Tuscarora System

The assault craft flashed into sight in the exit gateway. Conner turned to look at Black and asked, "Did this trip through the gateway take longer than normal?" Black tilted his helmet thoughtfully while he awaited the signal to exit the gateway. He received the signal and slowly moved the spacecraft forward. He continued monitoring communications and the surrounding traffic.

After they exited the gateway, he said, "No. It took the normal amount of time to travel between Susquehanna and Tuscarora. Now, take a deep breath and calm yourself. I think gateway travel bothers you a little bit, but let me tell you a secret. Gateway travel tends to unsettle almost all pilots of small spaceships. I am not sure why this is the case. I am not a psychologist, but I am willing to bet that it has something to do with the size of the vessel you are in. Gateway travel does not seem to affect very many people on larger vessels. Personally, I have found that a good way to keep your mind off if the traveling part is to concentrate on the ships surrounding you inside the gateway. I guess you could say that I'm more worried about the ships around me than about the process of traveling through the gateway." Now that they were clear of other ships in the immediate vicinity, Black shrugged his broad, armored shoulders and accelerated the assault craft. He then contacted the traffic control center onboard Tuscarora Station Three, which was the closest station, and requested to speak to the watch officer. To his surprise, he was denied. This was unusual. He then asked for an explanation, but he received no response. He thought about the situation and then decided to take a different approach. He asked Conner to contact the traffic control center. She had been listening to Black's brief conversation, and she was also confused by the response. She gave it a try and she was patched immediately through to Lieutenant Diamond. Upon hearing his voice, she pictured a weasel of a man. With their luck, all of the crew members of the traffic control center were probably weasels.

She sighed and replied, "This is UEF Marine Flight 256. We are requesting our point of designation." They already knew what ship the call was coming from. They also knew who she was, but formalities were necessary in official communications. Again, there was no reply. Ten minutes rolled by. Conner and Black discussed the situation. They were not sure if they had initially answered Conner because she was in the navy like them or because she was female. Black thought

Conner sounded like a hot babe. He figured she probably looked as hot as she sounded, but he had not seen her without her suit or her armor on. He probably would not admit to being attracted to her anyway. However, some members of the UEF Navy took offense to the presence of members of the UEF Marines. This was why Black had Conner make the second call. When she had first reported for duty with his squad, Black had been glad to find out that Conner did not seem to harbor any ill will toward marines. Personally, he did not see why there were rivalries between military services. Even when he was back in the US Marines, he did not understand why they had so much conflict with the navy, the army, and the air force. At the highest levels of the military, there was always conflict over military budgets and government funding, but he did not think that this was a major reason for the rest of the ranks to be at odds with the other services. This was one of his favorite topics to debate with his fellow marines.

After eleven minutes had elapsed, the traffic control center replied, "Marine flight 256, we have no record of your vessel, nor any orders pertaining to Master Sergeant Black or Spacer Conner. I think you are perpetrating some kind of hoax, and you might have hostile intentions toward military assets in this system. You are hereby ordered to change course and vacate this system immediately!" The two pilots turned to look at one another, and they burst out laughing. Fortunately, they were not transmitting their laughter to anyone else. It was nice to just laugh and relieve some of the tension that they had both been feeling over the past couple of days. After they were done laughing, Black felt like blowing up the control center in anger, while Conner felt like breaking down and crying. Black used his NCI to display and plot some calculations for traversing the system. He had been to Tuscarora many times. He knew where the testing space was in this system. He was not sure if that was where they were supposed to go for the trials. That was why they had contacted traffic control. Then he had a thought. Maybe he could contact the marine commander for this system. He was uncertain whether he would know where they were supposed to go, but it was worth a try. He spent another minute plotting different potential flight paths until he found one he liked. Then he uploaded the instructions to the vessel. The vessel changed course and he briefed Conner on his plan. She liked it and she agreed to it. Next, Black attempted to contact Lieutenant Colonel Hemprey, but he was unavailable. Black then asked Major Vohh if he knew about their orders. He also asked if Vohh knew where they should report for the training exercise. Black thought that perhaps he had miscalculated how the Seventy-Third

Battalion would perceive the Twenty-Third Battalion's invitation to a training exercise in their system. Major Vohh did not provide any information or help, but Black thanked him politely and ended the transmission.

Voicing the question that Black had been thinking, Conner asked, "Now what do we do?" The new flight path would take them to the gateway in the Sol System. He had chosen this path because it would take them closer to the location where the training exercise would most likely be held. They still had another hour before they would be within sensor range of that location. At that point they would be able to detect any military ships that might be there. He weighed his options again and decided to brief the rest of the squad.

Bloom, Riley, and Chin looked up when Black entered the Den. Black called Swartz and Kalam, interrupting their simulator training, and told them to join the rest of them up front in the den. Black and Conner joined them. "What is up, boss?" asked Riley. They all had their new armored suits on. The faceplates did not retract like many of the others, but Black was displaying a virtual representation of his face on the outside of his faceplate. Once they figured out how to do it, the others followed suit. They listened to Black's explanation of their arrival into the Tuscarora System.

He finished by saying, "In conclusion, I want to let you know about the current situation. I want to let you know that we may be delayed or blown up by friendly forces." Black shrugged like it was no big deal, which made Riley groan in despair. Bloom was hunched over his seat in his usual disgruntled pose. Before anyone had a chance to interrupt him, Black continued with his story.

"I am not sure whether the traffic control center on station three tagged us as unfriendly or not. I do know that they did not tag us as hostile. If they had done so, every civilian vessel would be running for its life. They would all be running away from us. We have roughly forty minutes before we are within scanning range of the testing space. At that point, we should be able to determine if there are any military vessels there. We may be able to contact someone who knows about our mission and knows where the hell we are supposed to go. If we are unsuccessful, I plan to wait until the next shift change before heading to Tuscarora Station One. There are bound to be some gold-wearing officers on Tuscarora Station One who are aware of the trial and our orders. Now, do you guys have any helpful suggestions?" Apparently, Black caught his tongue in time. The expression on Riley's virtual face made him look like he was going to speak. Then his mouth closed and a brief smile appeared.

Swartz asked, "How about sending an e-mail to Lieutenant Colonel Hemprey? If he is in the system, he will receive it. He should be able to a respond before we reach the gateway in the Sol System." Black nodded his bulky head.

"Yes, that is worth trying. Anyone else?"

Kalam waved his hand and said, "Do you know the name of the destroyer that had the crew that was using neural interfaces? Despite that they are part of the navy, they would probably be helpful and worth contacting." Black nodded his head while he tried to remember the name of the ship.

After a minute, he said, "*Ravager* is the name of the ship. That's a good idea, Kalam. I will have Conner keep an eye out for the destroyer. She seems to have slightly better luck communicating with the navy than I do. Apparently, my voice is not sexy enough." This comment elicited some groans and snorts of laughter all around the den. After this comment, it did not seem like anyone else had any other ideas. Black headed back up to the cockpit and joined Conner. He asked her to search for the *Ravager* and to attempt to contact the captain for further orders pertaining to the training exercise. Black checked the sensor picture in the area of the testing space, but the sensors were only reaching the inner edge of the area. So, he decided to implement Swartz's idea. He composed an e-mail and then sent it only to the system. If the Lieutenant Colonel were not in this system, then the message would eventually be kicked back to Black as undeliverable.

Two hours later, they reached the closest point near the testing space where they would not gain unwanted attention. However, Conner was still unable to detect any ships using passive or active sensors. Black turned the ship around and headed to Tuscarora Station One. In the meantime, he told Conner that he needed to get some sleep before they reached their destination. The fourth shift had ended an hour earlier. Hopefully, the annoying traffic controller at Tuscarora Station Three would not be a problem. Black knew some of the officers who would be on duty during the first shift on the first station, so he was fairly confident that things would improve.

Six hours later, Conner reached around Black's inert body and activated the controls on his chair so that it would move to its normal upright position. Master Sergeant Black woke up from his sleep. He thought about checking the status of the current situation on his neural interface, but he decided to just ask Conner for an update. She replied, "Well, sir, you were asleep for about six hours. Three hours ago, we started to receive orders from Lieutenant Colonel Hemprey on Tuscarora Station One. Commander Jha on Tuscarora Station Three and Vice Admiral Rayner on the first station contacted us next. The orders all conflicted with each other. After quite a bit of fuss, they agreed that two frigates would escort us to the first station, where we would disembark and stay until receiving further orders." Despite the fact he was nursing a headache from the new update, he focused on his neural interface and brought up the local sensor picture around their ship. Sure enough, two frigates were flanking them. He then checked to see when they would arrive at Tuscarora Station One. They only had thirty minutes before they would reach the station. Black asked Conner if she had told the rest of the squad the news. She said that she had not told them yet. It seemed like Black considered her part of the squad now. It filled her with a mixture of emotions, but she pushed down her feelings and tried to relax. She was startled a bit when Black asked her to give the squad the news so that they could prepare to dock in the station.

Chapter 11

Station One, Tuscarora System

E veryone in the squad except for Black and Conner, were asked a few questions by high ranking navy and marine personnel and quickly dismissed. They had not received any new orders. Without Master Sergeant Black, the squad members were unsure about what to do next. After a while, Staff Sergeant Kalam decided that they should get some good unhealthy food from the food court while they had the chance. The squad members tromped down to food court. They were still wearing their new battle armor, but their helmets were off and tethered to their sides. At first, some of the guys in the squad felt apprehensive about wearing their armor around the station. They worried about how people might react. Then they saw Staff Sergeant Kalam and Lance Corporal Swartz confidently and proudly wearing their armor. It was clear that it was an honor to wear marine uniforms. Bloom, Riley, Chin, Swartz, and Kalam had just bought their meals and found a table. They were in the process of removing their armored gauntlets, when Swartz's old-fashioned wrist communicator started to chime repeatedly. Swartz had to stop short of taking his first bite of a dripping triple cheeseburger. He growled menacingly at the interruption. He had an ear bud in his right ear, and he also wore a disposable microphone that was patched to his throat. Swartz always seemed to be talking to someone about his fleet intelligence work. He also sometimes handled the external communications on the assault craft. Swartz tapped a few buttons on his wrist communicator and barked an angry greeting. Since Swartz was angry, the informant kept his conversation brief. Swartz soon disconnected and swore under his breath. Although it was barely audible, the swearing piqued their curiosity about the nature of the information.

Finally, Corporal Bloom asked, "So, what is up, Swartz? Was that news about what is happening to our two wayward companions or has something else tweaked your shorts?" As he stared through his greasy burger, Swartz continued to mutter. The guys were about to lose interest and go back to eating their meals.

Then Swartz said, "No, it was not about the other two. Someone wanted to let me know that the information blackout regarding the trial had been lifted. The news of the combat trial is spreading like a fuel fire. It is no surprise that it is such a big deal. Admiral Rolands announced that the two new drone carriers will be on the center stage for this trial. Unofficially, the combat trial will be a match between the new carriers and a squadron of navy ships."

Chin looked at Swartz and asked, "What about marine forces and our specific squad?"

Swartz gave a small shrug in his bulky armor and replied, "He did not mention us or any other marines. My guess is that Vice Admiral Rayner plans to stash us on one of the destroyers. It will most likely be the *Ravager.*"

Kalam nodded in agreement, saying, "Yes, that would make sense. Originally, all of the navy ships were supposed to carry marines onboard, including support ships. These ships were similar to some of the wet navy ships on earth. I am not sure if you are familiar with the story, but all of this changed when we established the treaty with the Nubians and the gateways began to provide instant access to all of the systems that we explore. The UEF Marines became a police force because of the rapid expansion of infrastructure within the systems and the lack of governments and police officers. I have talked to the master sergeant about it, and he agrees that the current setup is not going to work for very much longer. Marines might be OK for security work. However, as you are probably well aware, it is just not possible for us to police civilians under the current laws." All of the guys around the table nodded. They displayed a wide range of emotions. They were all unhappy about the current state of affairs.

However, rumors were going around that the UEF was considering dismantling the UEF Marines. They were just glad to still have jobs.

The squad had just finished eating. They were halfheartedly discussing what to do next when a nearby commotion attracted their attention. A boy who was probably in his early teens was trying to run around the pedestrians. About ten meters behind the boy, a group of older teen boys was giving chase. They didn't look happy.

Swartz stood up from his chair and said, "I think I recognize that boy who is being chased. The staff sergeant introduced us the last time I was here on this station. I think Kenny is his name." He sighed, grabbed his garbage, and then headed toward the trashcan that was closest to the boys. The rest of the members of the group looked at each other and then back at the lance corporal.

Staff Sergeant Kalam stood up and said, "Come on, everybody. We better go after him. He'll either get beaten up by a bunch of boys or he'll get carried away and kill them all. The other four guys were soon scrambling to keep up with the staff sergeant. As they maneuvered through the crowds, they tried to not knock anyone down with their bulky suits of combat armor. If they weren't careful, they might crush someone to death. Leading the four men, Corporal Bloom became annoyed. He put his helmet on and activated all of his lights, including two intense floodlights. People started to scatter to get away from the blazing light. The four men caught up with the staff sergeant as they exited the food court and the common area. They headed down one of the corridors. Bloom shut off his lights. To be safe, he left his helmet on. It turned out to be a wise choice. Because as the five of them entered into the cargo bay through a hatchway, Bloom took a hit to his left shoulder from a stunner. It had no effect on the combat armor, but it got the attention of everyone else. They quickly took cover and put their helmets on. Unfortunately, they had no weapons. As long as they were only facing stunners, though, they would be OK. However, they hadn't expected this attack, so it was hard to know what else they might face. Just as things felt like they couldn't be any more uncertain, the power to the entire cargo bay shut off. As the lights shut off, the entire room grew dark. The gravity plating in the floor also shut off. Gravity immediately disappeared throughout the room. Cries of surprise and panic came from deeper in the room. The squad activated their magnetic boots, and they switched to the thermal optics so that they could see in the dark. They were now able to see the differing temperatures of objects and people. Chin looked over at some crates that were secured to the floor by some webbing material. He thought that he had caught some movement on the ceiling. Suddenly, a figure sprang from the ceiling to the floor. They heard another stunner being shot.

Speaking over the squad channel, Chin said, "There is something really big in here with us. I just saw it pounce down from the ceiling."

Riley growled and said, "Great. Those navy wussies don't want us to have weapons. Now we have to fight hand to hand. Never mind the fact that we are on the same side."

Staff Sergeant Kalam interrupted him by saying, "That's enough, private. We will just have to make due. A marine never is truly unarmed, though."

They all replied, "Hoorah!"

Thirty seconds later, three more shots came from the left side of the room. Ten seconds after that, they heard a boy screaming. Then they heard two more shots on the right side of the room. A minute later, the power was restored to the room and the squad started to move forward into the room. They made their way cautiously through the stacks of boxes, crates, and other assorted piles. It was harder to fit between the narrow spaces near the back of the cargo bay, but they managed it. When they reached the back wall, Kalam halted the squad. With the tiny cameras in the knuckles of his middle fingers, he cautiously checked around the corners in each direction. With a single thought, he placed both video feeds side by side at the top center of his HUD. The left was clear. On the right, though, something was barely visible on the floor. It looked like the bottom of a shoe. Meanwhile, Bloom was watching Kalam's back. Swartz was watching the rear, and Riley and Chin were watching the areas on the sides and above them. Kalam decided to search the right side first. As a group, they moved around the corner to the right, and they went into a small open area that bordered the back wall. To their surprise, they saw six boys lying on their backs in a row. Apparently, they were unconscious. On the other side of the open area, Master Sergeant Black was tending to a boy named Kenny.

After the men removed their helmets, Black glanced up, shook his head, and said, "What took you guys so long?" Riley scowled. Kalam shook his head and grinned in amusement, Swartz chuckled. Bloom looked disappointed. Chin was still looking around warily. Black finished attaching the bandage to Kenny's right arm.

"Are you OK, Kenny?" asked Swartz.

Kenny nodded and said, "Yeah. After diving to the deck to avoid a stunner blast, I hit one of the boxes and cut my arm." Swartz glanced at the pile of stunners on the deck that was across from the master sergeant. There were six stun pistols there. Black saw that Chin looked nervous.

He said, "Relax, Chin. No big aliens are going to pounce down and eat you today."

Chin shivered a bit in his armor and replied, "Are you sure, sarge. I could have sworn I saw something in there with us." Black sighed in resignation. This made the rest of the guys laugh.

"Chin, you have been watching too many alien horror movies. I was the one jumping down from the ceiling. I jumped down onto the leader of the boys. I disarmed him and shot him with his own stun pistol. It was easy after that. I just stalked down the rest of them and shot them with the stun pistol. I restored the power and dragged all of them back here so that I could keep an eye on them until you guys got here."

Chin asked, "How did you know we were coming?"

Black snorted and replied, "I saw your fat head poking out above those crates. I caught sight of you at probably the same time that you caught sight of me. All kidding aside, though, you did a good job spotting me. This armor blends in with the temperature of the surrounding environment. We probably only spotted each other because we were moving and our outlines were noticeable." Chin nodded and smiled. He looked relaxed. The master sergeant shrugged and said, "Besides, I was listening to the squad channel. I heard you guys chattering when you finally decided to put your helmets on."

Staff Sergeant Kalam winced and replied, "Sorry, master sergeant. I will not make that mistake again. I will make sure the guys have their helmets on the next time we run into any trouble."

Black waved his hand, stood up, and said, "Relax, Kalam. I am sure all of you did not expect them to be armed with stun pistols. Frankly, I am still surprised that they were able to get their hands on them. Kenny here is not sure where they got them from, but he thinks that some criminals might be hanging around the station. Anyway, Swartz and I will keep our ears out for trouble while we are here. In the meantime, Kalam will be a kind gentleman. He will order your servants to carry these boys off to the detention center in Section 6-27. Captain Donaldson is waiting to give you your gifts. This includes the stun pistols. The captain promised to pass the word along. Station personnel will investigate this incident. For now, I am going to escort Kenny home. I will meet you in the lounge in Section 2-12." Black looked at Kenny and asked, "Is that correct?"

Kenny nodded and said, "Yep. The new navy guys were bragging to my dad about their new fancy carriers. All of them were heading up to the lounge." Black looked down, smiled, and roughed up Kenny's hair. He waved at the other guys and headed off with Kenny. The squad put their helmets back on before they started to load up the boys. Chin and Bloom slung a boy over each of their shoulders, while Swartz and Riley each carried one of the boys. Kalam carried all of the stun pistols. On their way through the station, the group made quite the show.

Black went to the ship, picked up his duffel bag, and headed to his temporary room on the station. When he got there, he quickly undressed and jumped into the shower. After being confined inside of his armor suit for a couple of days, it felt good to be immersed in the massaging spray of the shower. However, he had to cut his enjoyment short. He needed to get up to the lounge soon. He decided at the last minute to wear civilian clothes. He was not on duty. He figured that he might garner less attention this way. Finally, he stuck a disposable throat microphone to his neck, and he placed an ear bud in his ear. He removed the interface adapter from his helmet and attached it directly to a spot on his neck that was behind his right earlobe. According to the manual that he had read for this particular device, he could apparently use the interface adapter to connect to any wireless device on his body. He decided to give it a try. He left his room and headed to the lounge while he ran through the necessary procedures to setup the adapter. After a few minutes, he heard an annoying buzz that was followed by a beep. This was supposed to signal that the connection had been established. He performed a speech test into the microphone. A few seconds later, he was surprised to hear his message repeated. It felt strange for him to perform mental tasks that he would normally be able to visualize. He was sure that it had its limitations. He could imagine that making a mistake could get ugly really quickly. Black decided to conduct a real test by trying to connect to the squad channel. "This is Black. Does anyone hear me?"

A few seconds later, the staff sergeant said, "Yes. I hear you, master sergeant. Is everything OK?"

"Yeah, everything is OK. I am testing a new communication setup. However, I forgot to mention earlier that our room assignments are posted on the squad's network. If it is not too late, you guys might want to stop by the ship and take your stuff to your room."

"No, it is not too late. As always, you have perfect timing. We just finished handing the prisoners over to the captain, and we were about to head up to the lounge. Thanks for the timely update." Black chuckled and said, "OK. I am just arriving at the lounge now. I will see you guys in a bit."

"Hello, Rachel!" Rachel Conner looked over at one of the tables in the lounge that she had just walked into. She saw her cousin, Diane Hope, bubbling with enthusiasm and rushing toward her. She braced herself. Sure enough, Diane ran up, gave her a big hug, and almost knocked her over.

"How have you been? What have you been up to? You do not look well. Have you been eating enough food? You really should try this diet that I am trying. You aren't married yet, are you? No? Well, are you at least dating? There are a lot of cute guys in here tonight. Maybe you should ask one of them or all of them for a date." Diane winked and then abruptly turned around and started walking away from her. Rachel panicked at first because she thought that Diane was going to start asking guys to date her right away. However, much to her relief, Diane just seemed to heading back to her seat at the table. Rachel looked around and spotted Master Sergeant Black and his squad in the corner of the room. They seemed to be enjoying themselves this evening, despite the reaming she had heard that Black had received earlier. She wandered over and sat across from Diane. It was now apparent that Diane had been drinking wine. She was intoxicated. Her behavior was not abnormal, but Rachel noticed that Diane was a little tipsy. This was probably why she had made a beeline back to her seat.

Rachel eyed Diane and finally asked, "So, Diane, what brought you to Tuscarora?" Diane waved her hand and put her wine down. In her intoxicated state, it seemed to be a bit taxing to operate both hands simultaneously.

Diane answered, "Oh, Auntie Susan invited me to visit and to report on tomorrow's big battle. Are you going to be there? You must go! It is going to be a lot of fun. Stuff will be blowing up everywhere."

Rachel shook her head and said, "Nothing is going to blow up. It is only a practice battle."

A guy who was wearing a brand-new navy uniform at the next table said, "Hey, darling. I could not help but hear you two lovely ladies talking about tomorrow's battle. If you want, you can come cheer for us." Rachel sighed and tried to ignore him, but Diane had to make things interesting.

Diane smiled at the man and asked, "Where do you want us? Are you going to be on one of the ships?" The guy actually puffed out his chest, which made his friends laugh.

Slurring his speech a bit, he said, "Well of course, darling. I am one of the crew members of one of the best, newest carriers." He got up, stumbled toward Diane, and tried to grab her. Rachel had just stood up. She was about to move toward the man to intercept him, but in a flash Private Chin was standing between Diane and the navy man. Chin held his hand up and stopped drunken man in his tracks. The man tried to brush Chin's arm away, but Chin knocked him back slightly and blocked his progress again. Rachel then blinked and noticed that the rest of the squad was standing around their table in a defensive formation. She was about to tell them that she could handle things. Then the rest of the navy guy's buddies got up and rushed over to the marines. Rachel shook her head in amazement. All eight navy guys were flattened to the ground within seconds. As with most navy and marine altercations, things did not end until some officers step in to restore order. However, every drunk or hotheaded navy crewman and officer was fighting with Black's squad. Likewise, another table of marines jumped into the melee for some fun. Rachel looked around in horror as the lounge was quickly trashed. She then heard a man clearing his throat. She turned around to find Master Sergeant Black cradling an unconscious Diane in his arms. She looked at Diane and then she scowled at Black.

"What?" asked Black. "She passed out and slumped onto floor. I did not want anyone to trample on her or injure her. Can we get out of here?" Rachel relented a bit.

She asked, "What about the rest of your squad?" Black shrugged.

"Eh, I will let them have some more fun. They need to burn off some steam. I'm not letting them drink any alcohol tonight, so they are not happy. They will be fine, though. They can handle this crowd. Can you make a path for me and lead the way to Diane's room." Rachel sighed, nodded, and led the way out of the lounge. Well, it definitely had been an interesting evening.

Deep Dark

Chapter 12

Navy Testing Space in Galaxy Space near
the Tuscarora System

On the morning of the battle trials, Spacer Conner found Captain Donner eating breakfast in a lounge that overlooked his ship, the *Ravager*. She was still confused about the events of the previous day. She felt like a clueless pawn. The debriefing from the day before had been conducted in the presence of many navy officers, including Vice Admiral Rayner. After receiving a lot of questions, Vice Admiral Rayner had provided Conner with many assignments to choose from. However, she did not feel disappointed about remaining onboard *MAC 256*. She had had a rough start, but in the end she had enjoyed performing her duties onboard the little ship. Oddly enough, she also enjoyed working with Master Sergeant Black. He was a great instructor and leader. Now, she was curious about how he would perform in a combat situation. Finally, she had asked the vice admiral if it would OK for her to wait to choose her next assignment. She asked if she could remain onboard *MAC 256* until the trials had been completed. The vice admiral was a professional at hiding his emotions, so Conner did not know whether her request had puzzled or annoyed him. Internally, he was still hoping to win her over. He wanted her to volunteer for a position with his personal staff. However, Captain Donner had mentioned that her request might work out well. Master Sergeant Black had also requested for Spacer Conner to remain onboard for the combat trial. This time, Rayner's reaction was visible. Conner saw him gritting his teeth with annoyance when Donner said this. In the end, almost everyone in the room agreed. Rayner made it official but he decided that he wanted Conner to inform him about the next assignment that she would be taking. She hesitated for a minute. Then she asked if she could be reassigned to the *Ravager* after the trial had been completed. The vice admiral gave a stiff nod and then walked out of the room without saying a word. Conner guessed that the vice admiral had wanted her to become one of his staff drones. However, she was now hoping to find out why Captain Donner had mentioned the master sergeant's request in the meeting. She was startled when he answered her unprompted. "So, spacer, you are wondering why I backed up your request to stay onboard the marine assault craft." He looked up at Conner's shocked facial expression and chuckled.

"Relax, Conner. I cannot read your mind. You had a bewildered expression on your face when you were walking up to me. I took a stab in the dark as to the nature of your confusion." He glanced up at her again and she nodded slowly. He said, "I have crossed paths with Master Sergeant Black a few times, and I found him to be equal parts scary, smart, and cunning. I think that this would be a good opportunity for you to learn from him. I am just glad he is on my team this time."

Conner's eyebrows rose in surprise and she asked, "Are the marines fighting with the *Ravager*, sir?"

Captain Donner replied, "Oh, you have not heard. Yes, three navy destroyers will be fighting against two new carriers. Each destroyer will have two marine assault ships to use as they see fit. To be honest, I am not sure how useful they will be. The navy is providing the refitted assault craft so that they can use it on a trial basis. My opinion is that they are nearly worthless in their current configuration. The marines have it rough enough with the navy brass offering nails for their coffins."

Conner then asked, "What do you mean? I did not think that this trial really had much to do with the marines." The captain replied, "Well, it is no real secret that the council of the United Earth Federation has been debating whether to disband the marines completely. The odds are that the outcome of this trial might just decide the fate of the UEF Marines."

Swartz gave Conner a warm greeting by waving at her as she approached their substitute assault craft in the hangar bay of the *Ravager*. "Welcome to *MAC Double-Oh-Seven*, spacer." Conner stopped and laughed at the ship. It looked pitiful.

"Does it fly, lance corporal?" Swartz rubbed his chin, looked back at the ship, and shook his head.

"Probably not. All that matters is that it hold atmosphere, right?" He looked back at her, winked, and then waved her closer to the ship. "Instead our normal double-rail gun turrets, this beauty is armed with simulated first-generation pulse laser turrets. Even if these lasers were shooting at full power, I doubt that they would cause any harm to any military vessel. However, the master sergeant just commented that it would not be much fun if the navy did not make it challenging for us. I am sure he meant no offense to you, ma'am."

Conner waved her hand and said, "He is right, lance corporal. Word has it that some of the navy brass would like for the marines to disband. They probably want to get their hands on your funding after you are gone. It is kind of sad, but I guess they call that politics." Conner pointed over to the front of the ship and asked, "What are Riley and Bloom doing with that foil on the front there?" Swartz turned to look.

He scratched the top of his head and replied, "I have no idea. The master sergeant told them to cover the front with foil and duct tape." He shrugged. "I have no idea why he told them to do this." He turned back to Conner. "Do you need help carrying anything onboard the ship? We will be finishing up here in about ten minutes. For the purpose of this trial, we will be staying onboard the assault craft as the *Ravager* gets underway. Then it will take a couple of hours to get to the testing area. I am not sure when the trial will officially start, but I guess Captain Donner will announce it when he finds out."

Conner nodded and asked, "Where is the master sergeant? Is he already onboard?" Swartz nodded and explained, "Yeah, he is in there cursing up a storm. If you can believe it, they actually installed the new neural interface in the cockpit of this garbage scowl. You and the master sergeant went through all of the trouble to get it working on the *MAC 256*, and then they tell us to use this piece of junk."

Swartz shook his head in disgust and said, "I will never understand the mindset of the brass."

Conner smiled, shrugged, and replied, "Well, I can kind of understand the logic behind that decision. We were kind of late to the party. Someone probably figured that it was easier to upgrade this ship than to switch out the weapons on our ship."

Swartz snorted with amusement and said, "Listen to yourself. You are referring to the *MAC 256* as our ship. I guess this means that you want to join our crew permanently." Conner's eyes grew huge and she started to stutter. Swartz just roared with laughter and then walked off to the front of the ship to check on the progress of the work that the members of the crew were completing there.

Two and a half hours later, all of the ships indicated that they were ready at their designated starting points. From her flag bridge onboard a cruiser called the *Rampart*, Vice Admiral Colder opened a channel to all of the participating ships. "Welcome, everyone. You have all worked hard over a short period of time, and I thank you for your diligence and dedication to serving the UEF Today is a momentous day. Today, the UEF Navy unveils its newest addition to its growing fleet. Behold, the new drone carriers, *Alpha* and *Bravo*." Black snickered at the grand announcement. Conner elbowed him from the copilot's seat. She was struggling to scowl, but she kept smiling and laughing.

She said, "*Alpha* and *Bravo*. Wow. That is original. Think about it. All of the brainy people are in the navy. Heaven help us all."

Conner snorted and replied, "You are smart and you in the marines." Black shrugged a bit in his bulky combat armor and replied, "I fudged the entrance exam so that I would make it into the marines. I started as a marine in the United

States Marines. I was planning to stay in the marines when I decided to give the UEF a try."

Conner shook her head and said, "I am still not sure if I believed that the entrance exam is rigged, but I will believe your story for now." When the vice admiral's speech was over, Conner started to remind everyone of the rules. "When a ship's simulated damage reaches between 60 percent and 90 percent, the ship becomes disabled. Disabled ships will not be able to operate systems at random. When more than 91 percent of a ship becomes damaged, we consider it to be destroyed. For the remainder of the exercise, these ships will not participate in the action. The carriers both have beacons located in their engineering section, their combat information centers, and their bridges. If the marines are able to board a given carrier and activate all three beacons, it will be considered captured. Likewise, it will not participate in the action for the remainder of the exercise. The exercise will end when all of the destroyers or carriers have been destroyed or captured. The drone and assault ships do not count toward the final outcome. The squadron commander for the destroyers is Vice Admiral Rayner. He will be onboard a destroyer that is called the *Hammer.* The squadron commander for the carriers is Admiral Rolands. He will be onboard a carrier called the *Alpha.* Now, fight with courage and honor! Begin the trial now!"

The three destroyers fired up their engines and began to accelerate toward their targets. Five hundred kilometers on the other side of the testing area, the two carriers were still holding their stationary positions. However, they were belching out clouds of drones. Each carrier was capable of holding six hundred drones, and Admiral Rolands had decided to launch all of them to attack the squadron of destroyers. Black opened a channel with his mind to the communications officer, who was up on the bridge.

"*Ravager*, this is *MAC Double-Oh-Seven*. I am requesting permission to launch." Ten seconds later, there was a reply.

"*MAC Seven*, you are clear to begin your launch cycle. *MAC Five*, you will launch in five minutes." Black warmed up the engines as a tractor towed the assault craft to the launch bay. The tractor stopped and disconnected. A minute later, the doors to the hangar bay closed behind them. After another minute, the atmosphere had been evacuated from the launch bay. The outer doors began to open. When they were halfway open, Black fired up the bottom thrusters. He lifted the ship off of the deck, nudged it forward, and gently glided through the opening doorway. After clearing the destroyer, he pointed the craft up and in front of the *Ravager*. He checked the sensor feed from his ship and his group. He saw that the drones were just now becoming visible ahead of them. A few minutes later, Sergeant Long, who was onboard *MAC Five*, contacted them. Long confirmed they had launched and were proceeding with their plan.

Conner opened a private channel with Black and asked, "So, what is the plan?" A request to display a window popped up in the display in her helmet. She accepted. She saw that the window displayed an isometric view of the battlefield.

Black then explained the plan, saying, "We are currently heading a ballistic course to this point." A dot flashed for a moment on the window display. "As you can see, we will be positioned directly above the advancing drones. At that point, we will change our vector and we will maneuver to this point." Another dot flashed between the drones and the carriers. "Now, I want you to double-check my math. This point is the critical one. This point." He flashed the second point again. "This is where the communication laser to the center formation of the drones should be located. To change our vector again without hopefully being detected, we will have to intercept their communication laser. We will have to disperse it and confuse their sensors. After that, we just follow the laser back to the carrier. We will have to knock out their sensors when we get within five hundred meters, and we will have to open the door so that the members of *MAC Five* can board one of the carriers with us."

Conner replied, "It sounds like a crazy plan, but if it works it will be a stroke of genius."

Black chuckled and said, "It is crazy. I am not sure if I would try something like this under real combat conditions, but I am fairly confident that it will work. I was worried that the admiral might hold some drones back in his reserve. Even worse, I was worried that he might use some of them for defense. Apparently, though, he is confident that sending all of the drones in one massive wave will wipe out the destroyers."

"Is that a possibility? Even if your plan works, it will not do us much good if we capture one ship and lose when all three of the destroyers are wiped out in the meantime." Black was quiet for a moment as he performed some simulations. Conner was beginning to wonder if Black would respond.

Then he said, "You are right. I was hoping that the destroyers would be able to attack and destroy the carrier that we were not going to capture. However, since the carriers are holding their positions, I do not think that the destroyers will be able to get within range before the drones disable and destroy them. So, I would like your suggestions on how we can capture both carriers simultaneously. Think about it while I change our vector." Conner was incredulous.

"How does he expect me to think up a solution to this crazy plan?" she asked herself. She had no experience with combat or tactics. Was he just picking on her? Maybe he was harassing her because she was in the navy. She was upset one moment, angry the next, and finally just sullen. She glared at the screen and watched it for a couple of minutes. Gradually, she started to calm down. She started to think about the current situation. She looked at the position of the carriers, and a thought popped into her head. She looked over at Black and asked, "What is the significance being within five hundred meters of the carrier?"

Black replied, "The scanners on the navy ships do not work very well when they are scanning the area close to the ship. They are unreliable between the hull and five hundred meters away from the hull. The common theory is that the scanners interfere with the engines or some other gear. To my knowledge, no one has attempted to fix the problem."

Conner thought for a moment and then said, "OK. But why were you planning to knock out their sensors if we would already be situated within the interference zone?"

"We would knock out the sensors so that Sergeant Long could get in close without being detected," he explained. Then he showed her a simulation of the plan. "As you can see, the carrier we will be targeting is beside and behind the other carrier. We will create a blind spot near the back. *MAC Five* can slip in closely through this spot. This carrier is blocking the other carrier's line of sight to this spot. At first, we only have to worry about this carrier. However, I think we will have to tackle the other one too. Do you have any ideas?" Conner scowled inside her helmet, but she tried to remain calm and focus on the problem. She panned back to the drones and then checked the line of sight with the other carrier.

"How about if we take all of the sensors as we move up to the front of the carrier. Then we can cross into the path of the closest communication laser from *Carrier Alpha*. We will also have to continue to fire on the sensors as we get to the other side." Conner waited while the master sergeant thought her plan over.

After a few minutes, he said, "Your plan sounds OK. However, I think we will forgo firing at the sensors after we pass the bow of the ship. *Alpha* will see us firing our weapons as soon as we are clear of *Bravo*, so we will just have to take our chances that *Bravo* will notice us closing in on *Alpha*. I do not see any other options at this point. Speaking of points, we are at the second point. Let me know if we intercept the communication laser." Five seconds later, the assault craft intercepted the laser, and Conner alerted Black. Black immediately and deftly shifted the vector of the ship to intercept *Carrier Bravo* along the path of the laser. Speaking into the squad channel, Black said, "I need two of you guys to man the turrets and take out the highlighted targets." Black then turned and looked at Conner. "Conner, I need you to try to locate *MAC Five* and send them a message about the change in plans. Make sure they know that they will be boarding and attempting to capture *Carrier Bravo* solo. Tell them that we will be attempting to do the same thing with *Alpha*. After we are clear of *Bravo*, give me a situation report regarding the rest of our squadron." As the ship was one kilometer away from the carrier, Conner heard Black mutter, "Now, I just hope the neural interface works as advertised. If it doesn't work like it should, we will be plastered all over the outside of their new shiny carrier." Seconds later, the assault craft was running parallel with *Bravo*. Privates Riley and Chin opened fire on the sensor pods on the giant carrier.

"All stations, report," bellowed Captain Odom over the wide communication channel of *Bravo*.

A lieutenant replied, "Sir, sensors on the starboard side of the ship are failing from stern to bow. The enemy appears to be firing weapons."

"Well, where is the firing coming from?" asked the captain. No one seemed to have an answer, so he called down to the CIC and asked again.

"Sorry, sir. We are blinded on the starboard side. On that side, we currently cannot detect anything, including the drones."

Captain Odom gritted his teeth and turned to the navigation station. Lieutenant Smidt said, "Roll the ship 180 degrees."

A tactical officer named Lieutenant Yarrow said, "Captain, I am detecting a possible contact moving across our bow and to our port side." The captain was really grinding his teeth now. Everything had seemed to be running smoothly, but now this fiasco was starting. If he continued to roll the ship, he would lose contact with the ship that had probably caused his problems. However, he needed the sensors to correctly use the laser communications with the drones.

He sighed and said, "Communications, contact the *Alpha* and inform them that a possible hostile contact is coming toward them. Tactical, provide the necessary information in the transmission."

"Damn. That was close!" yelled Conner as half a dozen screaming alarms turned on with flashing lights. "That was not close. That hit us. Well, it hit us slightly. We only suffered 30 percent damage on our ship, including the lower turret." *MAC Double-Oh-Seven* quickly closed in on its target and rolled so that Private Riley could fire the upper turret and destroy a couple of the defensive weapons near their target airlock. Black twisted the ship around 180 degrees and gently docked with the airlock. "We are docked, gentlemen. Bloom, crack the code. Conner, give me the situation report." Using a special device that was reserved for training purposes, Bloom went to work cracking the code on the airlock. Conner reported that the *Hammer* was destroyed and the *Claw* was almost disabled. However, the *Ravager* was still giving them a hard fight. All of the guys cheered for the *Ravager*. Conner smiled with pride.

After announcing that the airlock had been breached, Bloom said, "Conner, I want you to keep an eye on the ship and everything outside. I will be overseeing the capturing of the carrier and the controlling of the surveillance bots." Conner acknowledged these instructions and everyone went to work.

"Time to rock and roll, everyone!" Black said, turning on the music. All of the guys changed their external faceplates to display their combat faces. Bloom had the ghostly face of a wraith. Riley had a bloody skull. Chin had a black skull with purple, glowing eyes. Swartz's face looked the sunken face of a zombie. Kalam's face looked like a crazed clown.

"I have a pair of bots heading to each target location. So far, you are clear for the first ten meters. Head toward the bridge first and then work your way back to CIC and then to the engineering section. I will mark hostiles on your screens. Staff sergeant, it is your show now."

Kalam smiled and said, "Roger that. Let's move, men." The men quickly made their way through the ship. Once they had walked fifteen meters into the ship, the first red icons appeared on the screen, marking hostile enemies. They were around the corner that was up ahead, and they were heading away. Bloom moved quickly up. He stepped around the corner and stunned two crewmen who were about to go around the corner. Apparently, they were still unaware that the marines had boarded the ship. The marines made their way through the ship. Without an alarm being raised, they continued to surprise and stun all of the crewmen they encountered. However, it would only be a matter of time before someone encountered a stunned crewman who would sound the alarm. During this mission, speed was more important to the marines than stealth. As they reached the bridge, they found one of the bots controlled by the Master Sergeant accessing the door controls and hacking the entry code. When it finished, the keypad beeped and the doors hissed open. They moved in quickly and stunned anyone who looked like a security guard. Riley and Chin made a circuit around the bridge, and they located the beacon. Riley activated it and Staff Sergeant Kalam officially announced that the bridge had been captured. He asked Captain Hatfield if he had surrendered the bridge. It would have been unwise to stun everyone on the bridge, since this was only a combat trial. However, he had not been told to not stun everyone. If he had to stun everyone, he was prepared to do so. Captain Hatfield acknowledged that he was surrendering. Admiral Rolands, who was standing beside the seated captain, looked like he was about to pop a gasket.

Kalam heard Black say over the squad channel, "Go on ahead to the CIC I will keep an eye on the bridge crew." The staff sergeant nodded to the captain. He then followed Bloom and Swartz out of the bridge.

As soon as the door closed, the admiral said, "Communications, alert the CIC and engineering that the marines are on their way." The junior lieutenant looked like she wanted to be anywhere but there, but she looked toward the captain. Fortunately, she did not have to worry for very long. The power disappeared and the room went dark. Black backed the bot away from the emergency switch that would shut off the power.

He grumbled, "Two can play at that game, admiral."

Conner groaned, looked over at him, and said, "What did you do? Am I going to be called as a witness to your court-martial?"

Black snorted and said, "Why would you be a witness to my court-martial? You are watching the exterior of the ship. Not that there is anything to see here in the cockpit. I am only using my superior mental prowess against our enemies." The squad laughed in reply and shouted out all kinds of good-natured insults. A few minutes later, Black opened the door to the combat information center. He used one of the bots again. This time, the marines stunned everyone and then activated the beacon. As they left, Black brought up the rear of the squad with the two bots from the CIC. This was probably a good precaution, since the alarm started to wail. This spurred the marines to run at double their normal speed. They went to engineering, where they engaged in a brief stunner firefight. Thanks to the imagery that the hovering bots provided, the squad members were able to engage the crewmen without getting hit. They quickly moved in, located the third and final beacon, and activated it. The staff sergeant reported that the mission was a success. Even though Black already knew that they had been successful, this report was a standard procedure. They recorded everything so that they could examine it all in the future. Conner then told the group that Sergeant Long's squad had just finished capturing the *Bravo*. The *Ravager* had been disabled, but it had not been destroyed. However, the other two destroyers, along with the marine assault ships, were recorded as having been destroyed. So, we won the trial!" The guys all cheered. Swartz then started to sing their favorite rock song. Black quickly queued up the song to play over the squad channel. After they had calmed down a bit, Kalam asked a question that Black had been about to ask.

He asked, "How were the other assault ships deployed?"

Conner replied, "It looked like they were using the assault ships as screening vessels for their destroyers."

Swartz laughed and said, "What did they think? Did they think that the assault ships were gunships or something?"

"Yes. If they still had a dual rail gun turret mounted on their ships, their defensive fire may have been able to repel the attack. However, they did not have them this time. So, I doubt they lasted very long this time," said Black.

Chapter 13

Sol System

Americana Terminal - the western hemisphere's only gateway to the surrounding areas of space that were beyond the earth's atmosphere. The construction of this terminal had begun before any other orbital elevators had been built, but it had not been finished until a year after Triumph Terminal in Europe had finished being built. Due to public concerns surrounding the stability of the massive structure, the project had suffered many delays. Despite having been built in the middle of the arid geographical area along the border between the United States of America and Mexico, many activists had protested its construction. Eventually, architects, designers, and engineers modified the design of the lower portion so that it included twisted braces. These braced would increase its stability without transmitting any potential seismic vibrations from the braces to the central structure. From a distance, some people thought that the tower looked like an uprooted plant. It had a central stalk and roots branching out of the bottom of this stalk.

On August ninth, 2157 at exactly three o'clock in the morning, three of the communication dishes on the Americana Terminal redirected themselves toward empty space. However, within the line of sight of these three dishes, a small ship started to communicate back to the terminal. The first set of attacks was aimed at disabling the control centers of the terminal by disconnecting them from the computer network. The doors to the control centers, the security area, and the maintenance area were all electronically closed and locked. The next set of attacks as aimed at the residential sections. All of the residences were likewise sealed and locked. For the grand finale, all of the automated safety programs were deleted. Then, all of the external doors, including the hangar doors and the airlock doors, were unlocked and opened. As the outer hangar doors opened, the atmosphere was sucked out into the vacuum of space, killing everyone who was unlucky enough to be situated inside the hangars then. However, the attackers had not been aware that the Americana Terminal had been designed to prevent this kind of attack. The interior doors to the hangar bay disengaged their electronic controls. The dropping pressure actually sealed the doors. Airlock doors were scattered throughout the station. The rest of these doors were already closed. They had never opened. They only had remote locks. The doors could only be electronically locked from security centers or control centers. If the attack had succeeded, all of the corridors and open areas, including the terminal shopping and dining areas, would have been exposed to the vacuum of space. Everyone would have been killed. Because the attempt had failed, some of the off-duty technicians who were in the open public areas were able to tap into the network and fight back. Ben Adder was one of these technicians. He was able to trace the communications and overload the ship's antimatter power plant. The overload simply exhausted the power supply. It left the ship dead in space.

Emperor Terminal was undeniably the most beautiful orbital elevator that had ever been built on earth. It was possibly the greatest architectural marvel in the history of the planet. It was the first and only orbital elevator to be built over a body of water. In fact, the base of the main structure was connected to the bedrock underwater. Unlike the other structures of its kind, this elevator had an underwater annex for people to visit before and after they traveled to the terminal in space. The designers adopted a design that was similar to that of the Americana. Tendrils of tubes transported gyro-balanced bubbles that would carry passengers between locations all around Hong Kong. Unlike the Americana, the tubes and the entire exterior of the main structure was covered in layers of transparent composite materials. This allowed the passengers to see outside during their travels.

In the early hours of August ninth, 2157, three members of the cleaning staff found three strange objects in various locations. They found these objects within minutes of each other. They contacted security. They soon determined that these objects were potentially explosives, and they dispatched a team from the planet's surface to address the issue. The team disposed of the three bombs. Security forces scoured the terminal for more devices. They found four more devices, but they only disposed of two of them. The remaining two devices started to glow. The air surrounding them began to fill with static electricity. Then the objects began to resonate. Bolts of electricity began to spark from surfaces and from objects surrounding the devices. Finally, there was a bright flash. There was a popping sound and a dissipating sizzle. One security officer approached one of the holes that one of the devices had left behind. As he got closer, he could hear the ongoing destruction down below. Immediately, he notified his superior officer that some plasma explosives had been set off in multiple locations throughout the terminal. He told the officer that the explosives were burning their way down through the station. Security teams were sent to cordon off the damaged areas. The damage control teams tried to locate and extinguish the fires. They all thought that they had things under control. Then a member of the maintenance staff called in a panic, stating that the magnetic fields that slowed and stopped the passenger bubbles had all failed. The incoming bubbles were impacting the maintenance bay doors at the top of the shaft. Passengers were being killed on impact, and the damage was crippling the doors. If the doors were destroyed, the bubbles would then be propelled into the maintenance bay. They bubbles would possibly fly into the terminal beyond. Fortunately, communications were established between the terminal and the ground stations below. By cutting the power to the tubes, all traffic was stopped. Engineers and work crews would have to devise a way to quickly and safely get the bubbles down. They immediately began to work on finding a solution.

Triumph Terminal, which was nicknamed the European Tower, was the first orbital elevator that humans had completed. It started in the deepest man-made hole below the surface of the earth, and it soared into the sky. Its vertical, cylindrical structure extended up to the edge of the earth's atmosphere.

On August ninth, 2157 at 4:22 a.m. UTC, four passenger shuttles were each ferrying about a dozen people from the Triumph Terminal to various nearby orbiting stations. The pilots lost complete control of their vessels. They were unable to control their flight, and their communications were blocked. The external lights on the shuttles were extinguished, and their transponder ID cards vanished from everyone's radar. The first shuttle was sent flying into the top center of the terminal, where the control center extended above the entire complex. This effectively destroyed the entire nerve center of the terminal. Seconds later, the next shuttle collided with a massive fuel tanker that was floating near the terminal. It had been receiving fuel from refineries on the planet's surface. The massive explosion propelled the huge tanker toward the station. Automated safety control systems detected impacts on the station from debris from the explosion of the ship. This caused all of the elevators to automatically stop and shut down. In the end, this probably saved a lot of lives. The third shuttle had been heading toward the top of the elevator shaft, where the terminal connected with the shaft. The upper elevator maintenance hangars were also located there. A piece of debris struck the third shuttle, causing it to miss its mark. Damage from this impact caused the shuttle to explode. Its remains showered down and fell away from the station. The remains eventually burned up in the earth's atmosphere. The fourth and final shuttle had been targeting the residential ring. Travelers passed through this ring, and terminal staff members lived there. Its preprogrammed flight path intersected the incoming trajectory of the lifeless hulk of the tanker. The impact once again was fortunate for the Triumph Terminal. The tanker struck the terminal on the outside edge, causing significant damage and killing many people onboard. Only a small amount of the burning fuel made its way to the outside surface of the terminal. This fuel quickly burned away before any significant damage had been done. In the end, the attack had been brutal, but it could have been completely catastrophic for the prestigious Triumph Terminal.

Five hours after the attack on the Americana Terminal, Ben Adder received a call. He was told to drop what he was doing and to meet with his boss. At the meeting, his boss briefed him on the attacks on the other terminals. He said that police officers had surrounded the ship that Ben had disabled. The police officers were taking the cautious approach. They were waiting for the crew members to abandon the ship. Ben's boss then informed him that he had to help one of the police cutters apprehend the other attackers. They police officers believed that one ship was responsible for the attacks near the terminals. The authorities on Emperor Terminal were tracking a potential target, and it was heading toward the gateway to the Tuscarora System. Because of the substantial damage that had been done to the terminal systems, no one on Triumph Terminal was able to search for any ships. Ben's boss told him where to find the docked police cutter. Ben was finally dismissed. He grabbed a field tech kit on his way out of the control room, and he stopped by his quarters to quickly pack some clothes and other travel necessities. Fifteen minutes later, Ben boarded the cutter. He barely had a chance to sit down before the pilot told him to buckle up and hang on. The cutter left the terminal and quickly began to accelerate away.

Chapter 14

Tuscarora One, Tuscarora System

On the morning of the August tenth, 2157, Master Sergeant Black instructed his squad to transfer all of their gear from *MAC Double-Oh-Seven* to their good old MAC 256. The men were not happy about the assignment. They felt that the navy hangar crews should be doing this job. It was their duty to handle such things, but the master sergeant had insisted that they do it. The staff sergeant was all too eager to put the men to work. After almost three hours had passed, they were just finishing up. Two navy crew members of the *Ravager* stumbled into the hangar and ran up to three of their companions. They started to tell them something that made everyone excited. Judging from their expressions and gestures, it was not the good kind of excitement. The entire squad of marines had stopped to watch the spectacle, despite the fact that they were too far away and the noise from the various machines and tools in the hangar was too loud. Just then, the men heard a shout. They turned to see the master sergeant waving the squad over. They all obeyed and followed Black inside their assault craft. When they had all gathered in the crew compartment,

Black said, "I just intercepted some messages about some attacks in the Sol System." The news hit the men like they had been punched in their guts.

Kalam asked, "How bad was it?"

Black shook his head and said, "I have not heard anything official yet, but it sounds bad. All three terminals were attacked within hours of each other. From the sounds of it, Europe's Triumph Terminal got hit the hardest." The group was quiet for several minutes. They contemplated the matter, worried about loved ones, and tried to control their growing concern about their uncertain futures.

Private Riley finally broke the silence by saying, "Hey, sarge. What does this mean for us? I mean, what does this mean for our squad? Are we going to be sent back to Susquehanna, or are we going to going to Sol now?"

Black sighed, rubbed the back of his neck, and said, "I do not know yet. Obviously, we will go wherever we are ordered to go, but I have no clue where that may be." A feminine voice then broke in and startled the group. Rachel Conner and Diane Hope smiled widely. Black cleared his throat and asked, "What was that you said?"

Conner lost her smile and replied, "You are right, sergeant. We will be going somewhere soon. Until the admirals finish discussing the matter, we will not know where we are going."

Black's eyebrows rose and he asked, "Why are you saying *we?* Are you going to be staying with us?" He looked at Diane Hope. "I hope you do not mean that your cousin is going to ride along with us." He then turned to Diane and said, "Pardon me, but I do not mind carrying your drunken ass around, ma'am. However, this military ship is not a luxury boat. There simply is not enough space for passengers to join us." Diane just scowled at him and Conner. Conner had snickered and laughed at the mention of her drunkenness.

Conner then replied, "No. Diane will be staying on the *Ravager* for now. The ship she arrived on, *Proud Pegasus*, disembarked for Susquehanna yesterday. As far as I know, I myself will remain with your crew until I receive orders from either Vice Admiral Rayner or Captain Donner."

Black replied, "Well, I guess we shall see or hear what is in store for us shortly." The group then began to talk about other matters for an hour. Then the ladies had to go. The squad escorted them to the entrance of the hangar, where they said their farewells. On their way back to the ship, Kalam noticed that Black was eyeing the *MAC Double-Oh-Seven*.

"We are pretty much done unloading the ship, sarge. Is something else wrong?"

Black shook himself from his deep thoughts and replied, "Ah, I was thinking we could salvage some of the new gear that they installed on that ship. I doubt anyone will be using that ship anytime in the near future. While I could be sneaky about it and just steal the parts, I do not really want to risk endangering anyone who might be foolish enough to fly the ship without running through the checklist." He thought about the matter for a little while. Finally, he sighed and said, "Well, I think I will try to get permission for the equipment exchange."

Kalam snorted, waved his hand, and said, "OK, Black. Just let me know what happens when you are done." Kalam rounded up the squad and instructed them to finish transferring the last bits of equipment. Black donned his helmet and began to contact various officers to obtain permission to salvage equipment from the old assault craft. Most of the officers he was able to contact refused to discuss the matter with him. Disgusted with his results, he finally contacted Captain Donner himself. The captain thought for a long minute. Then he approved the request. He instructed Black to note in the maintenance logs that the equipment that they would be taking needed to be immediately replaced. Black was not really thrilled about noting this in the maintenance logs. It could come to back to bite him in the ass. However, since the captain was telling him to do this, he figured that he might as well take his chances. The navy personnel already hated the marines, so he was not worried about making enemies. However, after instructing Staff Sergeant Kalam to instruct the squad to strip and haul more equipment, he might become an enemy of his own squad. "Oh well," thought Black. "They need the exercise. They need something to do anyway."

In the evening, the *Ravager* and her crew were ordered by Vice Admiral Rayner to proceed to the Susquehanna. Further orders would be forthcoming. Master Sergeant Black and Sergeant Long now respectively commanded the marine assault ships 256 and 501. So, the two assault craft left Tuscarora One's hangars and docked belly to belly with the *Ravager.* They were then pulled into the destroyer and sealed inside of it. Nothing had been mentioned to Black about Conner's reassignment. So, he had her help him with some interface improvements that he could not manage by himself. In the meantime, Sergeant Kalam and the rest of the squad went to the gym on the destroyer. They worked out and they sparred with each other and with the other marine squad.

Just before noon on the next day, they reached the gateway in record time. They received their new orders at about this time. Their orders were to escort and assist *Police Cutter 49* from Sol. It was pursuing one of the ships that was suspected of attacking the terminals in Sol. Surprising, most of the navy personnel focused on the fact they would be chasing down the culprits. They did not focus on the fact that they were to merely assist the police. The police technically were not allowed to operate outside of the Sol System. The marines did not miss this fact, but the police had been rough on the marines in the recent past. Forgiveness was going to take a while. Master Sergeant Black was really annoyed. Then he heard about the police squad's plan. They planned to allow the cutter to travel to the Susquehanna System, where they would apprehend the terrorists. He was not pleased with the prospect of allowing the suspected terrorists to travel to Susquehanna, which he called home. Naturally, the police wanted to personally apprehend the suspects, but they had no good options for doing this. Police cutters could dock with other ships, but it was difficult when both of the ships were moving. It was especially difficult when one of the ships was not cooperating. Likewise, opening the hatch on the target ship would be extremely difficult and dangerous for the cutter. It might even be impossible. Black was pretty sure that one of the marine assault ships would be ordered to do this. This would explain why they had been reassigned to the *Ravager* in the first place. He was not sure why the admiralty had ordered two squads on this mission. Maybe the other squad would have to board the police cutter when they did not cooperate with the navy. Black grinned to himself. To complicate matters, the suspected ship had slipped into the gateway with a couple of huge transports. Ironically, one of the transports was the *Proud Pegasus*. The captain of this ship had apparently grown tired of chauffeuring Miss Hope around the galaxy. He had left to deliver her cargo to her company in Caledonia, and he had to travel through the Susquehanna System. It was a tight fit, but the *Ravager* managed to slip into the gateway with the two transports, the cutter, and the suspected ship. Fortunately, the transports were situated between the opposing factions. The *Ravager* and *Police Cutter 49* were stacked vertically on the left. The two transports were in the middle, and the suspected ship was on the far right. After a short wait, the automated Nubian gateway controller signaled the countdown for departure. As the countdown approached zero, all of the marines had finished putting on their combat armor. They were all strapped into their seats in their respective assault ships. They had not received orders to prepare their ships for action, but Master Sergeant Black and Sergeant Long both had a feeling that something was about to happen.

Chapter 15

Huntington System

Zeus flashed into existence on the edge of the Huntington System. Immediately, he began to scan the local space. Using the long-range scanners, he then spread his scans out. Courtesy of Tony Black and Infinite Machinations, he deployed several drones.

"So, what are the results of your scans?" asked Ethan.

"Well, our usual rendezvous point is at the large asteroid. This asteroid has a dozen detectable shuttles hiding on its surface. I am sending a few drones to investigate before we head in that direction. Well hello there! We just finished scanning the gateway to Susquehanna. Several armed ships are surrounding ten other vessels. Most of them appear to be cargo transports. There are several more armed ships around the gateway too. My guess is that they are stopping and apprehending all traffic that is coming through the gateway. Maybe they are just stopping what they consider to be unauthorized traffic."

Ethan interjected, "Armed vessels? Are you sure? Are they UEF forces or did Huntington create its own security force?" Zeus continued monitoring the results of the scans as he answered Ethan's questions.

"I am sure that they are not UEF forces. According to their size and configuration, I would classify them in human standards as corvette ships."

Ethan scratched the stubble on his cheek and said, "I have no clue what a corvette ship is. What is it?"

Zeus apologized and said, "Ah. Sorry, Ethan. The UEF Navy only designed one corvette ship, but it never put it into production. Tony told me about it. It is basically a military patrol ship that was designed wholly for in-system use. It is about half the size of a destroyer. It has half as many armaments. Because of its size, it does not have any docking bays. So, there are no shuttles, fighters, or assault ships. Tony told me that the police in Sol might acquire some corvettes soon, but the navy has no interest in the design." Zeus continued to monitor the information from the constantly updating sensor data. He also watched the progress of the various drones he had scattered nearby, as well as the drones that had sent toward the asteroid. However, these drones were still an hour away from reaching their target. Zeus and Ethan waited in silence as Ethan mulled over the current situation. Taking into account what they might find and what they already knew, Ethan tried to develop a plan.

An hour later, the three drones had reached the asteroid. They had already made two orbits around it. They used their sensors to map out the surrounding space and the surface of the asteroid. "The scanning is complete," announced Zeus. "There are actually fifteen vessels. From all indications, I am fairly certain that they are maxed out with passengers."

Ethan grimaced and replied, "Well, that sucks. I was expecting more refugees, but not that many. Based on the size of the ship, just how many refugees would you expect there to be?"

"I guess about eight thousand," responded Zeus.

"Wow. That many! Do you have any suggestions about how we should proceed?"

Zeus pondered the problem before saying, "There are three major problems. The first problem concerns the life support onboard those ships. At maximum capacity, they will not be able to maintain their life support for very long. The second problem is speed. We could attempt to leave the system with all of the ships. Five of them are huge transport ships. They accelerate at an incredibly slow rate. Because of their size, they stand out like huge beacons on everyone's scanners. The corvettes would have no trouble catching up to those ships before they reach light speed. We could split up. However, there is a third problem. It involves supply. If we decide to travel at the speed of light, we might run out of supplies like water, food, and fuel. Even if they stay hidden on the asteroid, they will face the same problem. The only way that they won't face this problem is if they smuggle supplies out of there undetected. However, it is doubtful that they can do this, and it would be risky. I currently do not know how to handle all of the problems, but I suggest we make contact and get more information before we waste more time considering the matter. We are not even aware of the current situation with the corporations or the corvettes." Ethan grimaced again but he nodded in agreement.

"Yeah, I agree. I guess we need to do that next. Go ahead and try to communicate with one of those ships. I will do the talking once you establish communications with them. Is that OK with you, Zeus?"

"You can do the talking. I do not mind. It is usually best for you to do the talking. I might use incorrect language and cause more problems for us." Zeus paused for a minute then continued, "OK, I made contact with one of the big transport ship. Be forewarned that we might have to refocus the communications laser on another ship if we need to talk to someone specifically. This will take some time to change." Ethan thanked him and began to talk to their first contact. Her name was Rebecca Cameron. She was the captain of the transport, Long Hope. She explained the current facts about the situation in the Huntington System.

Apparently, the largest corporations in the Huntington System had decided that they were tired of waiting. They decided to declare their independence from the United Earth Federation by seizing all of the ships in the system and taking them over with their own loyal personnel. Rebecca was not sure about what they intended to do with the ships, but they apparently killed some of the crew members who had not been completely cooperative. This caused panic and rage among the other crew members of the ship. This resulted in total chaos. Hoping to avoid the corporate thugs, ships took off in every direction. One corporate thug was foolish enough to fire on and destroy a ship that belonged to a distribution company that was simply in their way. The company, Orbital Nexus, demanded a cease to the hostilities. They also demanded compensation for the personnel, the ship, and the cargo that they had lost in this unprovoked attack. A system-wide broadcast stated that all companies that opposed the new Huntington government would be seized. Their personnel would be incarcerated. Naturally, this only made things worse. Complete mayhem and anarchy ensued. Cargo bots from Orbital Nexus collided with stationary corvettes at the space docks. They crashed into some small shipyards, where more of the corvettes were under construction. For the first time in the history of mankind, a full-blown corporate war was in progress. Rebecca explained that some of the ships had secretly planned to rendezvous at this asteroid. Ethan asked about the conditions of the ships on the asteroid. Rebecca had heard that the smaller ships were loaded to the max with people, but she was unsure of the current situation onboard all the ships. However, her ship was loaded with organic food from Solar Hydroponics, which was based in the Caledonia System. Rebecca recommended some people and some ships that they could contact for more information. Ethan thanked her and ended the conversation.

Ethan laid the back of seat down and started to rub his temples. "Are you all right, Ethan?" asked Zeus. Ethan responded by sighing and shaking his head. This made him wince.

Several minutes later, he finally replied, "Sorry, Zeus. The horrible news gave me a migraine. I have trouble thinking about this stuff without my head feeling like it will explode."

"Please don't do that. Your exploding head would make a huge mess. It would take forever for the bots to clean the mess up." Ethan snorted and laughed. He was a bit surprised that it did not hurt to laugh and he said this to Zeus.

Zeus explained, "Stress is probably causing your blood pressure to skyrocket occasionally. You are probably getting migraines as a result. If you plan to contact more people, I suggest that you take a break and relax for a bit." One hour and one meal later, Ethan began to talk to more people. He eventually arranged a formal meeting onboard the Long Hope so that they could discuss the situation and figure out how to remedy it. Right before he left for the meeting, Zeus stopped him and told him that he had detected a group of ships in deep space between the systems of Tuscarora and Susquehanna. Ethan asked Zeus to keep tabs on the ships. He said that they would discuss the matter when he got back.

Chapter 16

Between Tuscarora System and Susquehanna System

The gateway convoy flashed back into normal space, but instead of reappearing in the Susquehanna System, they had apparently dropped into the middle of nowhere. Captain Donner immediately put the *Ravager* on alert. He ordered the marines to return to their assault ships. The convoy then received a message to surrender. "Captain, the message appears to be coming from a ship that is situated off of our stern and port," said the communications officer.

"I concur, captain," said the tactical officer. "There appear to be two more ships of a similar size on our starboard side, but I cannot provide any more information than that. The commercial transports are blocking most of our sensors. However, I highlighted them as *Tango Two* and *Tango Three* in the tactical window."

The captain replied, "I see them. Thank you."

The communications officer said, "Captain, I have intercepted communications between the suspected terrorist vessel, which we are calling bogey one, and the ship that ordered our surrender, which is *Tango One*. They are warning them of our presence and of the presence of the police cutter." There was a pause.

Then the officer said, "I just overheard the unknown captain ordering his ships to attack us." The captain did not waste any time.

"Navigator, move us away from the civilian vessels. Tactical, disable the engines of the terrorist vessel if you can." The captain then opened a channel to the hangar bay and ordered the assault craft to be launched immediately. He then opened a channel directly with Sergeant Long and Master Sergeant Black.

"Gentlemen, I want the ship on the port side to be captured, along with the terrorist vessel. I do not care if you disable or destroy the other two ships, but deal with them before you attempt to board any of the ships. Is that understood?"

The marines answered in unison, "Yes, sir!" The captain had one final thing to tell them.

He said, "Be careful and good luck." Then the outside hangar doors opened. Both of the assault ships dropped down and took off in pursuit of their prey.

Long said, "Black, I think I am best at disabling ships. I plan to go after *Tango One* first. Next, I will go after bogey one. Can you handle the other two?"

"Of course. However, I plan to prove you wrong. You are not better than me at anything," replied Black.

Long guffawed and asked, "Do we want to place a wager on that?"

"Yeah, sure. But let's take it to our squad com network so that our misfits can join in," replied Black. Some plasma burst past *MAC 501*, nearly hitting the assault craft.

Long gulped and replied, "Yeah, that is probably a good idea. Things are heating up for us over there. Watch out, Black. They have plasma cannons." Black acknowledged Long and then disconnected his communication channel with him. Black then increased the speed of his ship as he finally came out from behind the last transport. Ahead of him and above him, *Tango Three* was apparently maneuvering to go over the top of the transports. Meanwhile, *Tango Two* was apparently situated in front of the transports. Presumably, it was there to block their path forward. This was a foolish rookie mistake, but Black was not going to complain. Black plotted a course down below the plane that the transports were currently on. He would circle around behind *Tango Three* and then come up directly behind *Tango Two*. He looked over to Conner, who was quietly sitting beside him and monitoring all of the systems. They all had their suits and helmets on, so Black opened a channel with Conner and instructed her to take over the flight controls. He then explained that he would let her know when to employ evasive maneuvers. He assured her that he knew what to look for when they were about to fire. Otherwise, he needed the ship to be steady while he engaged the enemy ships with their rail gun turrets. He then launched two electronic warfare drones. He hoped that the use of E.W. drones would be successful. Otherwise, this might get ugly.

"Is all of this rolling really necessary?" asked Private Yeager. Sergeant Long's ships were perpetually moving in a clockwise rolling pattern. He periodically used a random thruster to evade the constant barrage of plasma and lasers that was coming from *Tango One*. So far, they had not been hit. Because of his random maneuvering, though, they were off course and all of his squad members were ill from the spinning and the erratic movements.

The sergeant unclenched his jaw for long enough to say, "Shut the hell up, Yeager! As long as we are in one piece, I do want to have any backseat pilots." He paused for a moment while he checked the range. "Cunningham, we are in range to fire our rail gun. I am sending you a counter over the net with the countdown to fire. Keep a steady lock on the target to disable it and then fire when it reaches zero. You will have only five seconds to fire both rounds before I resume our evasion. Am I understood?" Corporal Cunningham took a deep breath to ease her stomach.

Then she said, "Yes, sergeant. I will attempt to disable their propulsion first. I have not been able to identify the type of ship, so I am not sure where the other systems are located yet."

Long grimaced and replied, "I understand, Cunningham. Do your best." He checked all of the displays to make sure that there were no impending disasters. Confirming that everything was satisfactory for the moment, he initiated the countdown and began to reverse the spin. Then he changed their vector so that it was closer to the target. Then he accelerated at maximum thrust just before the countdown had reached zero. At zero, Cunningham fired both rail guns in rapid succession.

Cunningham yelled, "Go." Long was already thrusting laterally.

"All right, Cunningham. It is your turn. Notify us when you are ready to fire. I will try to keep us on a steady vector so just give me a five-second warning. Keep it random so that they cannot time our movements." Cunningham grinned to herself and acknowledged his instructions. The first round hit its mark. The target barely evaded the second shot. The damage from the first shot had destroyed two of its five main thrusters, and the damage caused its automated systems to cut off the fuel to all of the engines. However, the damage did not affect its power or weapon systems. *Tango One* finally hit *MAC 501* with a burst of plasma. The plasma struck the lower front corner of the marine ship. Within a minute, it had destroyed two nearby thrusters and melted into the hull. Eventually, the lack of fuel in the vacuum of space extinguished it. The structural damage was minimal, but the loss of one forward thruster and one belly thruster was a major blow to its ability to maneuver effectively. Long tried to compensate by rolling the ship slowly and only firing the top and side thrusters. With this approach, he could evade getting shot and maintain a steady vector toward the target. Less than one hundred kilometers from the target, Cunningham obtained reliable thermal data from the target. She pinpointed a hotspot near the center and the top of the ship, but it was not in their line of sight. The rail gun turret needed a direct line of sight to hit its target. They needed to maneuver to get the shot. Cunningham relayed her request to Long. As he evaded the shots, he began to work the ship into a better firing position. When Cunningham had a clear line of sight, she signaled the five-second warning. She fired the first shot, confirmed her lock on the target's location, and then fired the second shot. The textbook shots hit exactly as planned. The first shot penetrated deep into the ship and breached its main reactor. Fortunately, it was not an antimatter reactor. The second rail gun followed almost the same exact path as the first shot. It passed through the exploding reactor and out the other side of the ship. The ship had no power whatsoever, and it was adrift in space. The remaining thrust came from the escaping atmosphere from the massive breach in the hull of the ship. The crew of *MAC 501* was finally able to relax a bit and relieve some unnerving tension. Then they refocused their attention on bogey one. In all of the excitement, they had not noticed that the police cutter and the *Ravager* had taken care of bogey one. However, the *Ravager* was still under attack.

Sixteen minutes earlier, Black was within fifty kilometers of *Tango Three*. He had also identified the reactor hotspot. His ship was on a lower system plane than the target, which was directly above the closest transport. Black pondered his options. Finally, he decided to attempt to use the E.W. drone to attack the target electronically. The other drone was currently being used defensively. It was corrupting the sensor readings of the two enemy ships and thus masking the assault craft's current position. It seemed like the two ships could not fire without locking on the target. Ever since Black had activated the defensive drone, the two ships had not fired a single shot. Black maneuvered the attacking E.W. drone on a ballistic course. This allowed the drone to remain undetected as it drifted closer to the target. When the drone was within ten kilometers of *Tango Three*, Black sent a signal via a communications laser to the drone. This process activated several automated routines within the drone. To determine if it could infiltrate the ship's systems, the drone at first tried to probe the ship's communications arrays. Finding a couple of accessible pathways into the ships systems, the drone began to insert worms into the vessel's systems. The worms found their way into the ship's main computer systems. They opened up bigger access points for the drone to utilize. Now that the drone had easy access, it began to viscously attack its primary systems, crippling the operation of the ship. The first targets were the weapons, which the worms disabled. Next, the flight controls were disabled and all of the fuel and power to the engines and thrusters was shut off. Third, all access points were sealed and locked. Finally, they searched the main computer and all of the major systems for important data. They relayed this information back to the drone and then to Black. Data files that were too big were hidden away in *Tango Three*'s main computer. Everything else was scrambled so that the ship would remain completely useless unless somebody installed the ship's operating system and replaced some key hardware components. Having continued onward to *Tango Two*, Black had Conner changed course so that they could get into the firing position of the reactor from above the target. To reach their destination, Conner had to use the thrusters to their maximum capacity. The resulting heat was enough for *Tango Two* to spot them. Black soon spotted the telltale signs of weapons charging at them.

Black yelled, "Conner, evade! Incoming fire!" Conner jumped into her seat at this unexpected shout. She quickly responded and started the evasive maneuvers. The first shots had all missed, Black instructed Conner to back the main engines off to 75 percent and maintain the evasive maneuvers. A second salvo was fired from *Tango Two*, but it did not even come close to them. Black instructed Conner to reduce their main engines to 50 percent and to stop evading the shots. When Conner complied, Black fired a single rail gun round at the center top of *Tango Two*. Black then noticed that *Tango Two* was powering up its weapons again. He wondered if the firing of the rail gun had been detected. He quickly checked the surrounding area. Then he spotted *Tango Two*'s target, which was the *Ravager*. The *Ravager* had moved in front of the transports so that it could engage bogey one at close range. It was now situated within firing range of *Tango Two*. *Tango Two* fired a full barrage of lasers and plasmas at *Ravager*. A round from Black's rail gun then struck the ship and obliterated its reactor, leaving it powerless and adrift. Meanwhile, the crew of the *Ravager* was rocked by multiple hits from *Tango Two*'s weapons. Both of the shots of plasma struck the lower front half of the ship, burning quickly inside the hull and breaching it. The air rushing out only further fueled the burning plasma, which continued to eat away and burn the hull, the electronics, the wiring, and the crew members. The ciders floated away into the deep darkness of space. The lasers struck the front and starboard sides of *Ravager*. The *Ravager*'s armor withstood most of lasers. There was some slight structural damage, but none of the lasers penetrated deeply enough to breach the hull.

"*Ravager*, this is *MAC 501*. What is your status? Please acknowledge." Sergeant Long waited for a minute before he attempted to contact the *Ravager* again.

Master Sergeant Black then said, "Long, this is Black. *Ravager* is disabled and adrift. I am now close enough. I have established contact with their secure network. Wait one moment while I check on their status." Five long minutes later, Black came back with a report. "Well, it is not good. The bridge crew and 5 percent of the crew members are incapacitated. A few of them are on the brink of death. There is also significant damage on the front of the ship. So far, there are twelve dead or missing crewmen on the *Ravager*. My copilot and I might be able to aid the incapacitated crew members and fix some of the damage. Likewise, the police cutter has some helpful personnel, including a medic. They are planning to help. Soon, both of these ships will docking with the *Ravager*. I need you and your squad to begin boarding the ships. Start with bogey one. The remaining crew of police cutter forty-nine will join you shortly to oversee the whole operation. After securing bogey one, coordinate and dock with *Proud Pegasus*. After that, deposit any prisoners in their designated cargo holds. Please verify that the rooms are secure. After that, continue on to *Tango One* and repeat this process. *Tango Two* and *Tango Three* and are also disabled. My remaining squad members will secure them in the meantime. The other transport vessel, *Far Yonder*, will house the prisoners from *Tango Two* and *Tango Three*. You know what you are doing, so take your time and watch out for traps.

Thirty hours later, all of the marines climbed out of their armor. They fell asleep immediately from exhaustion. For the most part, the boarding actions had gone smoothly. The only crew members who did not want their ship to be boarded were on bogey one. Also, one of Long's marines had been wounded in the encounter. As a result, all five crew members of bogey one ended up dead. None of the tango ships put up a fight. Their life-support systems had either failed or they were on the brink of failure. In addition, most of their crew members were new to life in space. They did not want to try to breathe in the vacuum of space, so they surrendered. A team that included Black and Conner was able to troubleshoot the problems that had caused the crew members to become incapacitated. Black was surprised to find that all of the *Ravager*'s crew members who were operating the ship had been housed in immersion tubes and chambers. It was like the navy's version of the armored suits that the marines used. The only glaring difference was that the tubes were life pods that could be ejected out of the ship. This time, the problem with the tubes came from the sensory overload of combat data and electrical feedback caused by damage in the front of the ship. Three people were now brain dead. Two others were in comas, but the medical staff members were confident that they could be healed and restored to consciousness. The rest of the incapacitated crew members had regained consciousness. They had a wide range of symptoms that ranged from migraines to blurry vision. Captain Donner had been treated for a mild headache. He was now leading the conference that was dealing with the current situation and planning on what to do next. Halfway through the conference, Sergeant Black interrupted the conversation to report the information that his squad had compiled.

"Captain, according to information obtained from *Tango Three* and *Tango Two*, these pirates are all criminals from earth. Manuel Ortega led this group. He is a major player in the Mexican cartel.

More of these criminals are apparently on similar ships that the Nubian manufactured. They were supposed to hijack more transports at different locations." Sergeant Long raised his hand so that he could add more information to the meeting. Black grinned and nodded at Long, encouraging him to jump into the conversation.

"I queried my squad about Ortega, and they confirmed that he had been captured, along with some information that had been hidden onboard *Tango One*. The information indicates that Jean Lupin, who is known as the Butcher of Latin America, is leading a coalition of some of the more ambitious members of the major criminal organizations on earth. Their objective is to penetrate something that is referred to as Acadia. They plan to free their comrades who are imprisoned there." Long paused for a minute as he scanned all of the information on his tablet.

Finally, he looked back up to the surrounding group and said, "The rest of the information is kind of vague, but I think that they intend to take over this prison and launch the first pirate operation in the area of space that the humans occupy."

One of the lieutenants snorted and grumbled, "Do these ambitious bastards really expect to succeed with this crazy scheme?"

Captain Donner frowned and replied, "Yes. They would have captured the two transports if there had not been any members of the navy, the marines, or the police."

The captain looked at Sergeant Long and asked, "Do you have any information regarding how bogey one fit into this whole affair?"

Long shook his head, grimaced, and said, "Not yet, captain. My squad is still trying to sift through *Tango One*'s data and the personal effects of its crew members. I can make this a priority if you need me to." Long shifted uneasily in his seat as he awaited Captain Donner's orders. His squad was exhausted from the mental exertion of scanning seemingly endless amounts of data, documents, and pictures. They were also exhausted from a lack of sleep. They were used to patrol duty. When they were on patrol duty, they could sleep on a fairly consistent basis. However, Long did not need to worry. Captain Donner contacted several officers who were not at the meeting. He asked if they were available to assist with the efforts to gather information. After ten minutes, the captain reported that some crew members were available to help the marines analyze the intelligence. The meeting continued for another hour. After discussing their future plans, they dispersed. They either resumed their current assignments or they began new ones.

Three days later, they had formed a new convoy of six ships. The convoy included bogey one, which they renamed *Star Fury*. *Tango Two* was renamed

Determination. Tango Three was now called *Anarchy.* The convoy also included the *Ravager* and the two transports, *Proud Pegasus* and *Far Yonder.* The two marine assault ships were stowed away inside the transports so that the marines would be available to guard the prisoners during their impending trip. *Tango One* had been severely damaged, and Captain Donner had decided to salvage spare parts from it. Navy and marine crew members took anything remotely related to the military. They left the rest of the parts for the crew members of the transport ships. These crew members used their own small shuttles to ferry equipment and supplies back to their ships. Since the crew members of the transport ships would be assisting in the upcoming operation, the spare parts were their compensation. Under the command of Captain Donner, the new convoy set a course for the Acadia Star System, which was located midway between Susquehanna and Sol. It was also midway between Tuscarora and Saratoga. The information was sketchy, but apparently an old star catapult propelled ships from Sol to Acadia. Another catapult in Acadia took care of the return trip. After an exhausting search, no information could be found regarding the Acadia System. Captain Donner decided to have the convoy travel there. If these aspiring pirates were to successfully take over the facilities in the Acadia System, he would attempt to bluff his way in. Otherwise, they would simply contact the authorities and try to resolve this mess.

Chapter 17

Meeting of the Nubian Grand Council

There were many gateway disruptions between the systems of Tuscarora and Susquehanna, Susquehanna and Saratoga, and Saratoga and Sol. These disruptions led to the emergency shutdown of all of the gateways in the areas of space that the humans occupied. Even the gateway to the Nubian territory was shut down. However, just before it shut down, it sent an automated message to the Grand Council of Trade, which was located in an entirely different galaxy. The Nubian Grand Council was the central government for all of the Nubian tribes. The Grand Council had three divisions that would meet up, although each division dealt with their individual matters separately. The divisions dealt with trade, defense, and what basically translates as infrastructure. The message had been sent to the trade division because it normally dealt with matters concerning alien governments. Nubian communication technology was far superior to anything the humans had. Nonetheless, the message took four months to traverse the immense distances of space. The Grand Council of Trade reviewed the message and immediately called for a Grand Council session with all three divisions. They needed to discuss the new crisis. The chief magistrate of trade replayed the message for everyone who was present at the session. The chief magistrate of defense divulged information about some Nubian ships that were possibly missing. These ships, he said, might be involved in the matter. Their drive signatures had been detected at multiple locations throughout human space, including the space between the gateways that had been disrupted. There was a lengthy debate about the possible culprits. They argued about who was to blame and what was to be done. In the end, everyone agreed that they should hire one of their mercenary fleets to investigate and deal with any possible opposition. However, another debate broke out over whom they should hire. Members of the division of defense wanted to resolve the matter quickly. This left them only one choice: the Felidaens. Their fleet was capable of instantaneously traveling anywhere. However, the trade members did not want to pay high fees to the Felidaens. They preferred to deal with one of their regular groups of contracted mercenaries. Like most standstills, it all came down to what the members of the Council of Infrastructure would decide after they had thoroughly debated the subject. They finally decided to side with the defense. They recommended contacting the Felidaens first to see if they were available and willing to take on the task.

Three weeks later, the Grand Council received a message from the Felidaens. In the message, the high commander of the Third Royal Fleet of the Felidaens accepted their mission conditionally. He included a contract that specified the conditions. The first condition included the method of payment. They specified the type and quantity of rare metals that they required. The amounts were high but not unreasonable. Next, there was a clause that outlined how much they would be compensated for the loss of lives and property due to negligence on the part of the Nubians. This stipulation greatly upset the Grand Council. They took it as an insult instead of a warning. Finally, the Felidaens wanted to retain the right to salvage and/or seize the enemy's equipment. They also wanted to retain their right to capture and enslave enemy prisoners. Because of the time constraints, the Nubian Grand Council agreed to the terms, and they approved the contract.

Almost six months after the last gateway in the human areas of space shut down, the Third Royal Fleet of the Felidaen Sovereign, Queen Ceibo III, prepared to deploy to an unknown location in an unknown galaxy. A scout ship was selected to conduct the reconnaissance missions. The crew members of the selected ship were all elite scout troopers. They had a wide range of skills and backgrounds, but survival was their specialty. No matter what happened, they would strive to complete their mission and return with a report. A scout who did not survive and return was worthless.

Chapter 18

Acadia System

"**A**xis eight outpost, this is *UEFP Transport 522.* I am requesting inner-system access to resupply at the facilities at Axis Nine," said the captain of Jean Lupin's transport ship. Sitting in the bridge of the massive transport, Jean and the captain were awaiting a response. They were hoping that this gambit could be pulled off. Jean was fairly confident that it would work. To succeed in this part of his grand scheme, he had invested a lot of time and money into information and bribes. While they waited, he pondered what might have happened to Manuel Ortega and his three ships. It was obvious that Manuel had encountered some opposition. That was why he had sent the extra Nubian ship to ambush the enemies. He figured that if Ortega showed up, he would have to be replaced permanently. Jean refocused his attention. They had finally received a reply from the outpost. The captain played the message in the form of a holographic video in the center of the bridge.

"*UEFP Transport 522*, permission for access to the facilities at Axis Nine is granted for seven days. If you have not exited the system by that deadline, your vessel will be seized and impounded. Have a nice day. Transmission complete." Jean growled at the man's insolence. He wished that he could gut him. Maybe he would return later and do just that. However, they had more important things to attend to.

"Captain, set the course for the Axis Nine Prison."

For the sake of his own safety, the captain saluted and replied, "Yes sir, Master Lupin." The captain then turned to his crew and started to issue orders.

Thirteen hours later, they docked at an outer service pier of the Axis Nine Prison. The prison is located on one of three moons that still orbited a gas giant. Axis One is a space dock and refinery that was inside one of these moons. The other moon housed Axis Two, which was an unfinished shipyard. The construction on the shipyard had been postponed until the prison was completed. There had also been other delays. Both of the facilities were of great interest to Jean. He planned to finish building the shipyard so that he could begin building his fleet of pirate vessels to dominate the galaxy. That was for another day, though. Today, he needed to dominate the pathetic guards of this prison. Jean and one of his most trusted bodyguards, Micah, exited the ship and made their way to the inner airlock hatch of the gangway. Micah opened the hatch and talked to the guards on the other side. Finally, Micah motioned for Jean to exit through the hatch. The two of them continued onward to the main prison facility. After ten boring minutes of walking down empty corridors while scanners examined them at every secured hatchway, they finally reached the control room. They did have permission to access the control room, but he had acquired a special black box that would enable him to disable the lock on the hatch and open it manually. Micah was doing a very good job when one of guards shot him in the head with a blast of lasers. Jean tossed two flashbangs into the room. He then ducked back around the wall and waited. The bombs detonated. Crouched down, Jean rushed in and quickly shot everyone he could find until they were dead. The last person alive could not get her laser pistol out of its holster. Jean took advantage of the situation. He jumped on her and plunged his dagger into her stomach. He then watched and laughed with pleasure. As he twisted the dagger around inside of her, she jerked around with spasms. After one last cough of blood, her body was finally still and quiet.

Fifteen hours later, Jean had nuked the Axis Eight Outpost. He was feeling absolutely thrilled. Someone might have found a way to manually operate one of the weapon stations independently. To prevent this from happening, Jean disabled the rest of Axis Nine's exterior defenses. The rest of his ships had arrived safely. They were docking and unloading their pirate army.

Chapter 19

Entering Acadia System

Black, Bloom, Riley, and Kalam looked up as Conner ran into the ship and then stopped to catch her breath. "Is everything all right, Conner?" asked Black. Conner nodded, paused, and then shook her head in the negative. She paused and nodded again. She changed her mind and shook her head in the positive. Black looked at the rest of the group and said, "Well, I think that means that maybe everything is all right." The guys chuckled halfheartedly. So far, it had been the year of bad news. Tensions had been high on their long journey to the Acadia System. It seemed like everyone was just waiting for the next disaster to occur.

With her breathing under control, Conner said, "We made it. We have arrived at the Acadia System, and Captain Donner just sent his first glimpse of the system. I wanted to show it to all of you. I heard it's scary and spectacular."

"Scary and spectacular," muttered Kalam. "No wonder you could not make up your mind about whether it was good or bad news." Conner downloaded the data to the ship and displayed on the overhead holoprojector. To see the three-dimensional image correctly, she joined the guys in the seats along the wall. The images and the video were from two electronic warfare drones that the *Ravager* was using as scouts. They were transmitting their data from a laser communication network of drones to the *Ravager*.

"Vishnu, preserve us," whispered Kalam.

"Amen, brother," replied Riley softly. Bloom replied by making the sign of the cross. Conner just gasped at the awesome sight. It was indeed scary and spectacular. The sight before them revealed a triple star system that had a black hole in its center. It was slowly devouring the other two suns and everything else in the system. However, the entire view of the system was far from complete. The views of the suns were beautiful, but they needed information about the facilities in the system. This data was going to take a while to reach them.

Black said, "We are on the wrong side of the system." Everyone looked at him in puzzlement. Then they looked back at the display. Kalam was the first to understand what was going on. He nodded in affirmation.

Then he said, "If you check out the vector information for the orbital data, you can see that everything is in a circular orbit around the black hole. Everything is also synchronous. Until now, this was unheard of." Kalam scratched his head in bewilderment. Black changed the view so that they were seeing the system from above the orbital plane and looking straight down onto the plane. Using his data pad, he began highlighting the points of interest.

"As you can see here, everything is rotating in this direction. This is the only visible planet. It is probably the only one that still exist in this system." He pointed at the gas giant that was orbiting the black hole on the far side of one of the suns. Conner interrupted Black and stated that there was an incoming update of data from the *Ravager.* Black paused while Conner handled it. A minute later, the image changed. It was now clearer and more complete. Of the greatest interest to Black was the appearance of moons around the gas giant. He saw indications that artificial structures were on the surfaces of these moons.

"There is a message accompanying this update. Should I start it now?" asked Conner. Black nodded and sat back down. The message turned out to be a presentation from some of the crew members of the *Ravager* who had analyzed the data and imagery of the Acadia System. During the first twenty minutes, they discussed what Black had already briefly pointed out. Finally, they highlighted one of the moons around the gas giant. "We are 80 percent sure that this is the location of our target, which is the prison. We have been able to identify some ships moving around its proximity. This leads us to believe that the pirates have already attacked and probably captured the prison." They continued to provide information for another ten minutes. They mentioned a fact that Black had been planning to address. Their target designation was orbiting away from them. After the presentation had concluded, Captain Donner made an appearance.

"Master Sergeant Black, I am hoping that you and the members of your squad will have some clever ideas about what to do. As they previously noted, our quarry is slipping away. I do not feel that we can wait until it orbits back to us. While it is true that these pirates might have attacked the prison and breached its outer defenses, it is not clear if they have completely subdued all of the interior defenses. In fact, I believe that it is unlikely at this point in time. I would prefer to attack them sooner rather than later. If you come up with ideas on how to accomplish this goal, let me know immediately." Black immediately began to tap away at his data pad. The others watched and waited. They were stumped about how to accomplish the mission. Thirty minutes later, Bloom and Riley left to relieve Swartz and Chin from guarding the prisoners onboard *Proud Pegasus*. While they were there, they filled them in on what had happened. Swartz and Chin jogged into the assault craft. They eagerly examined the display of the Acadia System. An hour later, Black looked up. He looked exhausted yet excited as he held up his data pad.

"If we survive, I think that we can get there in a month and a half." The squad members slumped their shoulders in unison.

Black's plan took some explaining and some convincing. After one incredible long and tiring week for most of the military personnel in the convoy, the retrofitted *MAC 256* and its crew members were ready to launch. The retrofitting had been necessary to incorporate the parts of the FTL systems that had been salvaged from *Tango One*. They had been essentially tacked onto the outside of the ship. Holes were made into the armor and the hull to allow for the ship to be connected to the power plant and other systems. Then Black went on several solo test flights to test his theory under the current circumstances. When he was satisfied with the results, they encased the new modules in armor plating to help protect them. On the journey to Acadia, Black had been studying and experimenting with the technology that the Nubians used to travel faster than the speed of light. The FTL technology of their ships was different than the technology that the gateways used. They used similar principles, but this version allowed only ships to skim through the dark matter between the systems. Black was not yet sure about how the technology worked. He knew that the system manipulated dark energy to create a quantum field that surrounded the ships. This created a slipstream when the ships came into contact with the dark matter stream. They could then travel from one system to another faster than the speed of light. The technology for the gateways was different than it was for the ships. Black guessed that this was because of the power requirements. This was Black's biggest concern. He was not sure how much power it would take to operate the shipboard technology. However, he was not planning to use it for its intended purposes. After studying endless amounts of sensor data, he was fairly sure that it would be normal to navigate through the gravimetric maelstrom that surrounded the black hole. Secret experiments had been done while traversing the gateways. These experiments provided conclusive proof that the quantum field negates the effects of gravity. However, it seemed like gravity could interfere with or somehow affect the dark matter. This could explain how they had been ambushed. Black did not know exactly what had happened. He figured he would leave this explanation to the scientists. At the moment, he did not have the time to ponder this. He planned to use the quantum field to protect the ship while they traversed the system. It was far more complicated, but Black had already planned most of their journey. He had to troubleshoot any problems that might appear along the way. The convoy would journey around inside the system. They would travel along the same orbit as the gas giant, but they would move in the opposite direction. *MAC 256* would take a shortcut straight through the system. It would avoid the black hole enough to not be pulled inside.

Sticking his head out of the ship, Black yelled, "All aboard the *Acadia Express*!" The squad members groaned and shook their heads as they finished preparing to embark the assault craft. Diane Hope ran up. She gave Black a big hug and a kiss on the cheek. This surprised Black. She then hugged Conner, who smirked at Black over Diane's shoulder. It was Black's turn to shake his head and put his helmet on. If there was anything in the universe that he would never understand, it was women.

Two weeks into their journey, they reached the edge of the gravimetric maelstrom. Conner was generating the quantum field when the sensors alerted Black to the appearance of a ship nearby. Black blinked and then decided to play back the recording of the ship's sudden appearance. He was sure that it had not been there a moment ago. There was a lot of interference with the sensors, but it was unacceptable for a ship to sneak up on them. Why would anyone be in an area like this, anyway? Sure enough, the ship appeared through a fold in space.

Conner then surprised him when she shouted, "Damn! Part of the ship just exploded and it is drifting away."

Black pondered the situation and then replied, "Well, they are drifting out of the maelstrom. Let's intercept the ship and rescue them."

Conner looked over at him and asked, "What about the mission? You said that it was crucial to gather sufficient velocity to transverse the maelstrom." Black sighed. He tried to nod inside his helmet, but it was barely visible.

"That is true. I guess I will have to attempt my crazy plan B."

Conner held her hands up and replied, "Do not tell me. This time, it is better if I do not know."

Black shrugged and said, "OK. That is fine. It would take too long to explain anyway. Let's focus on intercepting that vessel. Turn off the power to the quantum field generator so the quantum envelope stops forming around the ship. Then fly us over to intercept that ship. In the meantime, I will brief the rest of the squad.

Four minutes later, they had latched onto the ship. They had cut a hole through its armor and its hull. Black was getting ready to send the bots inside. Something then flew into the assault craft and knocked the bots aside. As Black steadied one of the bots, he saw that each marine had been tackled by armored figures. They were definitely not human. Black growled, stood up, and reached around to the locker where the weapons were stored. He grabbed one of the new bioplasma rifles and powered it up. He left the cockpit and entered the crew compartment. He shut the hatch and stepped along the wall. In his mind, he selected "Hyper Chemicals." This gave him a serious dose of chemicals that allowed him to operate at a superhuman level for a short duration of time. Using voice commands, he began shooting bioplasma. Three figures slumped away from their wrestling partners. The other two broke free and charged toward Black. Thanks to the chemicals in his system, they appeared to be moving at a normal speed. They were moving so quickly that they otherwise would have been blurred. Black shot the one on the left, but his shot seemed to have no effect. Black released the rifle and let it drop to the deck. To his right, he saw that Conner had followed him. She was standing in the hatchway of the crew compartment. The figure on the right was aiming its weapon at Conner. Black dropped it with a powerful right hook. He then shifted his weight to his left, reached out, and clotheslined the figure to his left. It had been trying to get past him.

On the edge of going berserk, Black quickly turned around and yelled, "Conner, get your ass back up to the cockpit. That's where it belongs." He then whipped back around to his squad. They looked pathetic. They were still a bit shocked as they slowly stood up from the deck. "You sorry excuses for marines better get your asses over to the ship. You better have it cleared in under a minute or I will smack you all down like I did to these two." He pointed down at the crumpled figures at his feet. The squad members looked at each other and then scrambled to exit the ship. Black needed to burn off the chemicals before he could become rational again, so he started to carry the enemies to a small storage room. After cleaning out the storage room, he removed the helmet from one of the enemies. It looked feline. He locked the storage room and traveled back to the main cargo room, where he began reorganizing the supplies. When he felt that there was a sufficient amount of open space, he returned to the crew compartment. He checked on the status of the squad members. Only two minutes had passed. While the squad members checked out the other ship, he decided to unload its cargo. Before he left, he positioned two bots just inside the stricken ship. They would serve as sentries. For backup, he placed another bot in the crew compartment. During their search, the squad members found the five dead bodies of their attackers. After making this discovery, they rejoined Black to help him unload the ship. The chemicals had worn off, and he was struggling to keep moving. As they broke away from the crippled ship, Black apologized to Conner. He explained that chemical enhancements had affected his mood. Conner thanked him for the apology and the explanation. With the thrusters pushed to the maximum speed, Black skimmed the edge of the maelstrom. Then they entered the maelstrom again. Conner activated the systems for the quantum field.

"Is this your crazy plan B?" asked Conner.

Black laughed and replied, "Hell no! Plan B probably would have killed us." He then stopped laughing and said, "No. The so-called rescue did not delay us for very long. I decided to redo plan A. Plan B probably would not have worked. It would have just wasted more time."

Conner replied, "OK. I was just wondering." The gravimetric turbulence was starting to get bad. Black was having trouble keeping the ship on course. The quantum field had formed. It began to shield the ship. Conner was impressed and surprised that Black's theory was correct. Hopefully, the rest of this insane mission would go smoothly.

Chapter 20

Near the Gas Giant in the Acadia System

B lack was abruptly awakened by a warning alarm. He was still in the cockpit with Conner, who was piloting the ship. Conner shut the alarm off and then reported, "Sorry, Black. Another ship just dropped in on us to say hello." Black checked the sensor data and camera feeds to examine their new guest. He yawned while he stretched his limbs out.

He then replied, "It is OK. I know whose ship that is, and they are a friendly. I will have a private chat with them to find out why they are here." Puzzled, Conner acknowledged him but she asked whether she should stop or keep going to their objective. Black instructed her to keep going. The other ship would probably join them for a bit, but there was no need to worry.

"Black, this is Ethan. Can you hear me?"

Black rolled his eyes and replied, "Yes, Ethan. I can hear you. We are on a private channel. What are you and Zeus doing here?" Ethan cleared his throat and then said, "Well, Zeus and I just helped overthrow the corporate tyrants of the Huntington System."

Black interrupted him by saying, "Good for you two. I have been meaning to do that, but I have been busy lately. However, that does not explain why you are here."

"Well, do not interrupt me and I will explain the whole story," snapped Ethan.

Black sighed and said, "OK, but keep it brief. We are about to be detected by pirates and then I am going to have to do all that ugly combat stuff." Ethan ignored Black's joke and continued his explanation.

"Zeus has been detecting strange activity in this area. Some suspicious ships were situated between the gateways, and we tracked them back to this system. When things quieted down enough in Huntington, we decided to come here and investigate. We arrived at the edge of the system. Zeus detected this ship and some anomalous readings. We thought that you might be in trouble, so here we are."

Black chuckled slightly and replied, "Well thank you, Ethan. I appreciate that you had my back. It turns out I do need some help. I need to make a trade with Zeus for some information." Zeus then broke into the conversation.

"You know that I only trade information for information." There was a long pause. Black waited patiently. He had sensed some hesitation in Zeus's response, and he was hoping to sweet-talk the alien. Finally, Zeus nibbled at the bait.

"What did you have in mind, Tony?" Asked Zeus.

Black smiled and replied, "Well, you know I am pretty good with robotics. I have been thinking about making a body so that you can actually interact with people and move around. If that does not interest you, I have some alien technology that might interest you. However, I have not had the chance to examine any of it."

Zeus then asked, "What kind of information do you want?"

Black sent an image to Zeus and said, "I am hoping you can identify this species and provide me with any information you have pertaining to them, including their language translation database."

Zeus sarcastically replied, "Gee. Is that all, Tony? Do you want all of their technology designs too?" Zeus's antics with mimicking humans usually amused Black, but he was not in the mood for it this time.

"Just stop, Zeus. I am short on time and patience. I have five survivors of that species on my ship, and they will be waking up soon. They attacked us when we tried to rescue them, and I had to subdue them. I probably injured two of them pretty good, and I am sure they will not be happy with me when they wake up. So, I would appreciate some help. I would normally just ask this as a favor, but I know that your kind does not operate that way. I am willing to follow your rules and your way of trading. I know you normally trade information for information. While I could probably find some information for you, I currently do not have any information that you would likely want to trade your information for. Now, are you willing to trade?"

After a minute, Zeus replied, "Yes, Tony. I will give you some general information and a translation database regarding the Felidaen species. We will discuss the payment later. For the moment, you owe me." Zeus then sent Black the information and ended the transmission.

Two hours later, Black opened the door to the storage room where the Felidaens were being held captive. His squad members were loaded with weapons. They were poised and ready on both sides of the hatchway to the room. Black was more concerned that they would shoot him before being overrun again. Black looked around the room and saw a Felidaen flanking the side of hatchway on the inside. Another one was examining and possibly treating the other two, who appeared to still be unconscious. To show that he was unarmed, Black held his hands up and his palms out. It seemed like a ridiculous gesture. The ones that were injured the worst had received their injuries from physical blows, rather than from weapons. Black decided to give talking a try. So, he addressed the room in general.

"My name is Black. My rank is master sergeant, and I am the captain of this vessel. I would like to know the condition of your injured kin." Black waited for a response. The one-hour crash course that Black had received was hardly sufficient for fully understanding this species. However, he felt that he understood them enough to get by on this first encounter. The Felidaen that had been checking on the two injured aliens helped one of them up off of the deck.

He replied, "I am Catnine and my rank is second striker. I am the medic. This is our leader. She has some broken ribs but they are healing. Despite wearing head protection, my other kin has a concussion. Her head struck the floor. I have been unable to wake her." Black nodded. He wanted to shoot himself for his own stupidity. She probably could barely see him nodding, and she probably would not understand what this gesture meant anyway.

"That is an honorable report, Catnine. I will shortly assist you with medically aiding your kin." Black watched as Catnine twisted around a bit. She looked down and bowed her head slightly.

Black was trying to interpret her body language when the Felidaen at her side said, "How do you know about our language and our customs?" Black thought for a moment. He had a bright idea about how to deflect this question.

He smiled and answered, "Give me your name and rank, fur ball." While he did not normally antagonize people during negotiations, she had insulted him by questioning him before introducing herself. It was his right to insult her back and instruct her on proper behavior. However, things quickly got out of hand. At first, she started to growl. Then the Felidaen beside her surprised her by laughing at Black's joke. However, since the Felidaen that had been insulted was also in charge, she had the right to backhand her underling. In a flash, Black was gripping her wrist mere millimeters from the nose of a wide-eyed Catnine. "Give me your name and rank now!" barked Black. She tried to pull her wrist away, but she gave up and answered him with a growl in her voice.

"I am Durora and I am the commander." Zeus had given him information about this species. Black saw that the rank of commander was roughly equivalent to his own rank. He let go of Durora and stepped back a few steps. Then he readdressed her.

"Commander Durora, I require the right of kinship among your kin for rescuing you. In addition, I will provide medical aid to your kin and help you return to your holds." Black's statement seemed to stun them. Durora unexpectedly started to laugh and smile at him. Species did not matter. He would never understand women.

Four hours later, Black had introduced the Felidaens to his squad. They were discussing various topics. Mostly, they were talking about military stuff, including the reason why the

Felidaens had arrived in the Acadia System. Conner had been eager to talk to other women. Black was alone in the cockpit when the next alarm went off. "Incoming missiles, everyone. Buckle up. Conner, help the Felidaens secure themselves with cargo straps to the opposite wall. Then return to the cockpit." Conner acknowledged his orders and then explained the situation to the Felidaens. Black was busy berating himself for being sloppy and not launching the drones earlier. He had been busy but that was no excuse. It was a rookie mistake. Black maneuvered the newly launched drones into position. The two electronic warfare drones were positioned to provide a defensive screen. The communication drone was positioned to establish a link with the recon drone, which was scouting ahead to find the source of the launch.

Jean Lupin rushed into the control room and bellowed, "Why are these alarms going off? Someone better answer me or I will kill you all!" They erupted with a chorus of replies. Ortega pointed to someone who spoke Spanish. He yelled at him to repeat himself.

"Master Lupin, we are under attack. Rather, we will soon be under attack. Some of the automated defenses spotted a ship and they fired missiles at it. They destroyed the missiles and it appears to be heading this way. However, they are using some sort of jamming device. We cannot lock onto their ship." Lupin dismissed the man, who was unfortunate enough to have wet himself during the encounter.

"You need a target lock to fire the missiles and the torpedoes, but you can still fire the lasers and the plasma weapons manually. Do that and let me know when you have destroyed the ship." He then moved over to the commander's chair and sat down while he waited. Thirty-two minutes later, Lupin was about to start shooting the incompetent fools. One of them jumped up and cheered. They all watched the image of a ship. Because of a missile strike, it was venting atmosphere and debris. Apparently, the idiot who was jumping around had found a way to fire the missiles like simple dumb rockets. He had gotten a lucky hit. However, the ship was very close to them. Lupin and the rest of the people in the control room realized that the ship was going to crash into the facility.

"Destroy that ship!" bellowed Lupin. It was too late. The criminals were all scattering from the room and heading deeper into the complex. The ship crashed through one pier after another. The ships that had been docked there drifted away, spewing air and bodies. *MAC 256* crashed into the main complex and penetrated three decks before coming to a rest in a large dining hall.

Riley groaned. He shook off some debris and dust. He released his restraints and stood up shakily. He looked toward the space where the front of the ship used to be. Everything beyond the wall of the crew compartment had been crushed. It had all broken away during the crash landing.

"Oh no," said Riley. "Damn. Black and Conner. Did they—"

Kalam interrupted him. "No. I just checked the net. Black is still alive, but he is not on the ship. Conner—" A loud moan interrupted him. Conner removed her helmet. She was lying in a heap of cargo that was secured down with cargo netting.

"How did you get there, Conner?" asked Swartz.

"I think Black saved me, but it happened so quickly that I am not sure," replied Conner.

"Ah shit!" blurted Kalam. He checked the net again and cursed some more before voicing his fears. "Black has gone berserk." Some of the guys groaned, but Conner was not sure what the big deal was.

"What does that mean?" she asked.

Kalam replied, "I cannot explain. It is a secret but we are in trouble."

Conner scowled at him and said, "Black told me about the chemicals. Are you saying that he dosed himself too much in order to save me?"

Kalam blinked in surprise and replied, "He told you? Well, that is a surprise. That man is normally tight-lipped about that kind of stuff." Conner was about to snap at him when he held his hands up.

"Relax, Conner. Yes, you are right. He probably activated a very high dosage of hyper chemicals. I do not know why, though. He might just be pissed off at these pirates for trashing his ship. In fact, he is probably literally ripping them apart right now." Conner calmed downed a bit.

Then she asked, "So, what do we do now? I guess you are in charge now."

Kalam sighed and replied, "Well, I guess we have to go after him and try to recapture this prison. Conner, try to find some bots that still work. You can control them while we move through the complex. Bloom and Riley, check on the Felidaens and help free them. Chin and Swartz, check our equipment and start equipping everyone for heavy action." After an hour, the six humans and the five Felidaens made their way into the prison complex.

Deep inside the prison complex, near prison block four, the last five prison guards were still defending the access point to block four and the rest of the prison blocks. Six other guards were injured badly enough that they were unable to withstand much combat. They were still holding pistols, but they believed that they would not be able to provide much resistance. In the event that they were overrun, they thought that they might be better off shooting themselves. This would be preferable to rape, mutilation, and seemingly endless torture. The guards all straightened up and prepared for more combat. They heard a distant rumbling. Then they saw an armored personnel carrier entering the main corridor and heading their way. This elicited many groans, mutterings, and curses from the assembled defenders. They detected more movement at a corridor across the way, where most of the fighting had been occurring. However, as they were preparing to fire, the side corridor erupted with screaming and the firing of weapons. It continued for only ten seconds. One man skidded around the corner and ran toward their location. Before anyone could aim and shoot, a round from a rail gun splattered the man all over the opposite wall. The armored personnel carrier was only twenty meters from the cross corridor. To add to this excitement, an armored figure stepped out of the cross corridor with a rail rifle cradled in the crook of his right arm. The figure held up his left hand.

In a loud and booming voice, he said, "Stop the vehicle and surrender!" The guards could not hear his response, but they could hear some laughter. One of the guards then pointed out the fact that the figure was a UEF Marine. As most marines would attest, marines do not beg or plead for people to surrender. If they refuse the first time, they are fair targets. The marine brought up the big rail rifle with his right arm and fired a shot that tore off the roof access hatch. Still running, he dropped his rifle and leaped over the front of the A.P.C., diving into the hole that he had just made. More gunfire and screaming ensued for several seconds. Then the vehicle came to a stop. The marine leaped back out through the hole and hit the deck with a loud thud. The vibrations from the impact could be felt fifty meters away. The marine scooped up his rifle and then vanished. The guards turned and looked at one another. They were unsure about what had just happened. They did not know what they should do next.

Meanwhile, back in the control room of block three of the prison, Lupin and some of his men had just discovered the proper procedure to awaken and revive the prisoners from their hibernating states. They had only awakened twenty-five of the three thousand prisoners in block three when they heard the sounds of combat coming closer to the control room.

Lupin yelled at his men, "Two of you, run out there and see what is going on. We should make sure that the guards are pinned down and unable to attack us. It better not be some of the scum that we brought over here. They better not try to stab me in the back. Go now and report back!" Two of the men nodded and ran to investigate the sounds. A minute later, they ran back into the room.

"Master Lupin, a couple of squads of marines appear to be fighting their way to block three!" Lupin scoffed at the terrified men.

"We have thousands of men with weapons. What can two squads do?" The man tried to work some moisture into his dry mouth and throat.

Failing, he croaked as he said, "They have rail rifles, and they are obliterating the men left and right. There is nothing in this complex that can withstand a projectile from a rail rifle, so we are about to lose." Lupin pulled his pistol out and shot the man in the forehead.

"We will never lose. I never lose! Remember that, cowards!" He then stomped his way to the control room door. He stopped with slack-jawed amazement as an armored fist punched through the center of the doors. He heard the sound of grinding metal. A marine appeared in the gap in the door. The animated image of a flaming skull was on his faceplate.

"Drop your weapons and surrender!" boomed the armored figure. Lupin answered by raising his pistol. Black used the remnants of his high dosage of chemicals to sprint over to Lupin and with his left hand he chopped off Lupin's head as he passed the criminal mastermind. Black stopped just in time to avoid crashing into some control consoles. He turned around at the sound of weapons being dropped onto the deck. Apparently, the other men were confident that their leader was about to die.

Black rejoined the rest of his squad with only eight prisoners. Thanks to the assistance of the Felidaens, his squad had fared much better. The Felidaen scout troopers had slipped into the midst of the pirates. They disarmed the men by throwing them through the air so they collided with their comrades. When Black heard about how well they had performed, he personally thanked Durora and her squad.

Durora scowled at Black and replied, "If you want to honor us, you can provide us with a way home like you promised you would." Black thought for a moment.

He asked, "Are there any supplies on your ship that might help you get home?"

One of the other squad members answered, "Yes. We have gear and probes for communicating in space. Together, they are capable of establishing contact with our home system." Durora growled at her squad member.

Black ignored her and said, "I forgot to mention it earlier, but we were able to transfer most of your cargo from your ship before we left it. I am not sure if any of it survived the crash, but it is worth looking into." Without waiting for a response, Black headed back to the location of the crash.

A week later, a squadron of Felidaen destroyers appeared in the system near the gas giant. The squad that Black, Conner, and Durora were in commandeered a captured yacht and met up with the squadron. Durora presented her report to the squadron commander. Squadron Commander Misteen then interviewed Black and Conner separately. Finally, Misteen convened a meeting with Black, Conner, Durora, and the rest of her squad. Squadron Commander Misteen opened the meeting by thanking Black.

"Master Sergeant Black, I am honored by your actions in rescuing these scout troopers. I am pleased that you completed your contract with us without demanding compensation. However, I would like to offer you a contract."

"But we do not deal with contracts. We are not mercenaries. Why is she offering that?" Conner asked over a private channel.

Black replied, "This is what they are familiar with. However, I may know of something that they can help with."

Epilogue

Lafayette System

The squadron flashed into existence on the edge of the Lafayette System. It set its course for the main corporate station. "I do not understand why the citizens of this system would abandon their home world and government," Squadron Commander Misteen said to Black. They were onboard the bridge of a Felidaen destroyer that was called *Final Sorrow*. Black smiled sadly as he watched the external visuals of the surrounding space and pondered human behavior.

"Yes, I think humans are chaotic in nature. We seem to thrive on contradictions. We crave the attention of others, and we establish families, groups, and communities. However, we are also prone to having conflict with others. This gets worse as the groups get larger. It's a wonder some of our governments have lasted longer than a couple of centuries. When we met the Nubians, they essentially forced us to finally create a world government. It took us seven years to create the United Earth Federation. I cannot help but feel that the process was rushed and the federation is ultimately incomplete." Black sighed sadly and slumped his shoulders slightly. Conner walked up beside him. She placed her arm around his shoulders and leaned against his left side.

"Do you think the federation will survive this?" asked Conner quietly.

Black shook his head and replied, "I do not know. In some ways, I wish we could start over and create a new government that is more complete and fair. However, I do not think that this is realistic at this point in time. As the new government establishes itself, there will probably be a period of anarchy in human space." Black shook his head and sighed. Then he said, "I have discussed this matter with lots of people from all walks of life. Some people think that all of the systems should be independent. They want things to be the way that they are here in Lafayette, but they want this for different reasons. Some people think that this is far too dangerous. They think that this will lead to human space wars in the future. There are many different views and beliefs."

Conner looked at Black and asked, "What do you believe? What do you see for our future?" Black turned to Conner with a twinkle in his eyes.

"What do you mean by *our* future?" Conner blushed, spluttered, and finally attempted to shove the marine. Black did not budge. His boots were magnetically attached to the deck.

"You know what I mean. I'm talking about our future as humans." Black's smile faded. Deep in thought, he returned to staring through the display.

After a minute, he replied, "We are definitely going to have some rough times for a while, but I think that I have some ideas that might help in the overall scheme of life in the future." Conner was about to question Black about this mysterious proclamation, but Squadron Commander Misteen reentered the conversation.

"My communications officer has informed me that we have established contact with the target facility. Do you wish to speak to them now, Master Sergeant Black?" Black gave her an affirmative response. She directed him to a station on the bridge where he could communicate with the facility. Black then listened to the recorded message that they had earlier received.

"Unknown ship, this is Tachyon Enterprises Supreme Command Headquarters." That was mouthful. "This is a restricted area, and you do not have the clearance to enter this system. You are hereby instructed to leave or you will be destroyed." Black grunted in reply and then chuckled to himself. This was just what he had expected from these idiots. After the com operator instructed him on how to communicate on the channels and frequencies that he was familiar with, Black sent a message to some of his contacts in the system. He then said to the squadron commander, "If I am not mistaken, this squadron can jump deeper into the system and closer to our target."

Misteen thought for a moment and then said, "Yes, master sergeant. We refer to this as shifting. We can move closer instantly. I now have enough scans of this system to successful shift without colliding with any objects when we exit the shift." Black nodded and thanked her for the information. Another two hours passed before the first indications that his plan might work were revealed. External lights on several of the stations began to disappear as the power was shut off. The next event involved the immediate evacuation of the transports. They simply started to undock and scatter in every direction away from the stations. Finally, escape pods started to erupt from the stations where lights were still visible. This was Black's cue to move the squadron in closer. He had to end this illegal research and development. He had to end this rebellion. Black turned to Misteen and said, "Squadron Commander Misteen, would you honor me by shifting closer to our target? After all, the escape pods are clear of the immediate area. I would love it if you fired upon all of the target stations where the lights are still visible. I would love it if you did this until they are all destroyed."

Conner gasped in shocked and said, "We cannot do that, can we?" Black shrugged slightly. "I had been planning on doing this eventually. Will we get into trouble for doing this? Probably. It needs to be done, though. This is the only way that will result in the lowest number of causalities. This will solve most of the problems that the greedy and ignorant CEOs in this system have started."

Misteen made an inquiring sound and asked, "What is it that your fellow humans are making here that has upset you so much?"

Black grimaced and replied, "My government outlawed several technologies that they viewed as too dangerous. One of these technologies is independent artificial intelligence." It was Misteen's turn to bare her teeth in a grimace.

"Yes. I think I understand what your people feared from that technology. I know of several species that were wiped out by their own creations. I think that you are honorable and wise to stop such a thing from happening to your own people." The squadron commander then turned to order her bridge crew to begin the operation.

When the last of the escape pods had been launched, the squadron shifted closer to the stations. Black was impressed. Misteen had timed it well. The timing was tricky under these circumstances. Because of the immense distance that the light traversed, the visual location of the escape pods took a while to reach them. Once they had made the calculations, though, they were able to travel to these locations instantly. Without this technology, Black would have had to worry about physically flying. He would have had to figure out his own speed and the best approach to take. Black refocused his attention when Misteen addressed him.

"Master Sergeant Black, the escape pods are clear of the area. May I have the honor of destroying these facilities?" If Black was not mistaken, she sounded like she was really looking forward to blowing up the stations. So was he.

"The honor is yours, squadron commander." Misteen issued the orders and they all watched as the destroyers opened the doors to their weapon bays. They fired massive laser beams that absolutely devastated the target station in seconds. The weapons on the destroyer were all fixed and facing forward. Misteen targeted each station with a pair of destroyers. This sped things up. *Final Sorrow* was alone. Fifteen destroyers were in the squadron, and someone had to be the odd one out. Twenty-one stations were being targeted. Since the stations were laboratories, they were small compared to most of the other stations that the humans had constructed. In less then ten minutes, the targets were destroyed. Black sent another message to his contacts, and he instructed Misteen to shift back to Acadia.

When they were back in orbit around the gas giant in the Acadia System, Black began to say farewell to the Falidaens.

"Thank you and the crew of *Final Sorrow* for the honorable and timely completion of my contract." Misteen revealed a beaming smile. Black was pretty impressed with himself. He was becoming a pro at dealing with the Felidaens. Maybe he had a future as an alien diplomat.

Misteen surprised him by asking, "Are you forgetting something?" Before he had the chance to compose an answer, Durora and Catnine entered the bridge and walked up to them. Misteen nodded encouragingly to Durora. A sense of foreboding fell over Black.

Durora looked at Black, released her clenched jaw, and said, "I, Commander Durora, recognize your right to kinship among our kin, Master Sergeant Black." Black blinked and thought to himself furiously. This sounded official. He tried to recall what it all meant.

Then Misteen said, "May honor shine upon you, Lower Commander Black! You are now a member of our kin and this squadron." Black was speechless, but Conner was not.

"What! He cannot become a member of your crew. He is a marine in the United Earth Federation. He is a human. Can other species become part of your crew?" Conner gripped Black's left arm possessively, as though she feared that they would drag him away at any second. To Black's further dismay, Catnine came over and possessively wrapped herself around his right arm.

Black groaned inside. Then he straightened up. He had an idea.

He looked at Misteen and said, "I will agree to the arrangement if I am assigned to Durora's crew on one of your scout ships. As long as I can remain in this galaxy, I will agree." Misteen stared at him for a few minutes with a keen eye. She mulled over his request. Finally, she bared a tooth, displaying a crooked smile.

She replied, "Yes, I am willing to allow a temporary reassignment of the commander's troopers. You and your human companion will become permanent members of the troopers. In the end, the group will hopefully serve as a joint military group for our two species. I would like to discuss the matter further with you, but now may not be the time." She glanced at each of the women who were attached to Black. She smirked and then walked away. Black looked at each of the women. They were beaming up at him. Black closed his eyes in resignation. Oh boy. He was in trouble now.

To be continued in "Chaos in the Darkness"!

United Earth Federation Military Rank Structure

Navy Enlisted Ranks

Spacer Recruit
Spacer Apprentice
Spacer
Petty Officer Third Class
Petty Officer Second Class
Petty Officer First Class
Chief Petty Officer
Chief Warrant Officer

Navy Officer Ranks

Ensign
Lieutenant Junior Grade
Lieutenant
Lieutenant Commander
Commander
Captain
Rear Admiral Lower Half
Rear Admiral
Vice Admiral
Admiral
Fleet Admiral

Marine Enlisted Ranks

Private
Private First Class
Lance Corporal
Corporal
Sergeant
Staff Sergeant
Gunnery Sergeant
First Sergeant
Master Sergeant
Master Gunnery Sergeant
Sergeant Major

Marine Officer Ranks

Warrant Officer
Chief Warrant Officer
Ensign
Second Lieutenant
First Lieutenant
Captain
Major
Lieutenant Colonel
Colonel
Brigadier General
Major General
Lieutenant General
General